THE MURDEROUS MONSTER AND THE STONY GAZE

POINT MUSE COZY PARANORMAL MYSTERY: BOOK THREE

KELLY ETHAN

THE MURDEROUS MONSTER AND THE STONY GAZE - BOOK THREE

*There's a murder at the pet show, a monster on the
loose and a nosy librarian turned sleuth.
Let the mayhem begin...*

Xandie Meyers and Point Muse had settled into a
peaceful routine after a spate of supernatural
murders and mayhem. But the peace is upset with
the grand opening of Point Muse Springs Resort and
its drawcard event, the Supernatural Pet and
Familiar Show—S.P.A.F.S for short.

Not everyone is happy with the resort opening and
the pet show coming to town. A series of accidents,
hoof and horn disease and gastro plagues the
contestants. But when the competition favorite is

turned to stone and the show takes a fatal turn, the prime suspect is Amelia Harrow. Witch, Vet, pet show hater and Xandie's Aunt.

Xandie has no choice but to turn Sherlock librarian and go undercover at the pet show with a trash-talking pug named Colin. It's time to pet up, win the show and solve a murder...

Can Xandie survive long enough to navigate her freaky new world? Or will things that go bump in the night have her for a midnight snack?

Unlock the mayhem of *The Murderous Monster and the Stony Gaze!*

ONE

"It was just a little pinch." Elspeth Harrow, matriarch of the Harrow clan of witches, winked at her uptight granddaughter.

"A little pinch that could get you arrested."

"He was flattered. Even gave me his grandfather's number." Elspeth waved the small piece of paper like a well-earned trophy.

"Are we talking about the same thing? The fire that you caused with a witchy potion mishap?"

Elspeth hid the paper behind her back with a guilty twitch. "Yesss?" She drawled her word and smiled sweetly at Xandie.

Alexandra Meyers, aka Xandie, librarian to the supernatural Great Library of Alexandria, currently residing in Point Muse, Maine, covered her face with her hands as two burly firefighters marched past, munching on chocolate chip cookies. "Tell me that's a plain old cookie with nothing special added to it?"

Elspeth pasted an innocent expression on her wrinkled face. "Of course. There's no way their teeth will glow in the dark for the next week at all. That would be a dirty trick to play on such fine and fit young gentlemen."

Xandie growled in frustration. The haggish Harrow witch liked to play in the darker end of the magic spectrum. Her five foot nothing of a grandmother had an obsession with colorful wigs too. Xandie hadn't seen Elspeth's natural hair in months. Instead, she was a continuous parade of rainbow-colored wigs and bedazzled jogger suits. Her grandmother was a mayhem-loving but also slightly evil, formidable witch. No one crossed Elspeth Harrow unless they had a death wish or a good hex remover.

"Give it up, Xandie." Lila Harrow, baker witch extraordinaire, slapped her cousin on the back. "She'll always cause chaos. I think it keeps her from dying."

"That and the ground-down bones of the innocents she's hexed," Amelia Harrow, Lila's mother, sneered at Elspeth. "Seriously, you couldn't wait to burn down Harrow House until we'd left for work this morning?"

Aunt Amelia normally had a good grip on her mother's leash, but lately, Xandie's tall, no-nonsense aunt with the same, amber-colored eyes as every Harrow female, seemed tense and anxious. Her late mother's middle sister was always full of energy, and since her Harrow gift was communicating with animals, her work as a vet was the perfect job. But the last few days, everyone was tiptoeing around her. Even Elspeth, who normally loved antagonizing her relatives, was avoiding her middle daughter. Xandie shifted back a few paces, in case an exchange of friendly fire erupted between her grandmother and aunt.

"I wasn't intending to burn the house down. I was creating a masterpiece. Giving life." Elspeth cackled, and the wind picked up around the Harrow women.

"Dial the hag back, Mother. Or you'll get us run out of town with torches." Amelia rolled her eyes at her mother's antics.

"Creating what exactly?" Xandie frowned and searched their yard. You never could tell with Elspeth if her antics were for good or evil, and since the fire fighters had been at Harrow House for a good hour before she arrived, who knew what the eccentric witch had actually done.

Elspeth tucked the phone number away in her jogger pantsuit pocket and waved a hand airily. "Oh, this and that. You know how it goes."

"Yeah, we have the fire station on speed dial, so we know how it goes." Lila blew a raspberry at her grandmother and pushed a long, curly lock away from her face.

Lila shared the same amber eyes as the rest of the family, including Xandie. But she and Aunt Amelia were the tallest of the Harrow witches. Lila had inherited curves and her love of sugar from their Aunt Winifred, her mom's youngest sister. Winifred's daughter, Holly, was the complete opposite, with short, bobbed brown hair and a tiny frame. Xandie, on the other hand, height wise, was between her two cousins. With shoulder length hair in the same shade of rich brown that tended to frizz in damp weather.

"Not surprised Doll-face here has a thing for the hot firemen. She's a whole lotta witch."

Lila's forehead wrinkled as a husky male voice rumbled from behind Elspeth's legs. "Do you have a short firefighter hidden behind you we don't know about?"

Elspeth shuffled her feet for a moment. Then reached behind her and picked up something furry. "Surprise. Meet Colin. Our newest addition to Harrow House."

Xandie reared back and hid her face behind Lila. *Oh, God. It was so ugly.*

"Mother, what have you done?" Amelia, animal healer and vet extraordinaire, pointed a shaking finger at the hairy pug her mother held aloft.

Lowering the dog, Elspeth cradled him to her bony chest. "I gave Colin an upgrade. He'll be perfect for SPAFS now."

Amelia growled. "He's not your pet or familiar, and no sane, healthy animal should be within peeing distance of that horrible, archaic, abusive institution."

Xandie sidled away from the cover of her taller cousin and raised a hand. "For those relatively new to the supernatural world and Point Muse, what is SPAFS?"

"Supernatural Pet and Familiar Show. The most popular pet event on the supernatural calendar around the world. I follow the blog on the witch boards, and this year, it's Point Muse's turn to host the show. I can't wait." Aunt Winifred wriggled her plump booty up to her mother and tickled the pug under his chin. "Aren't you the cutest boy? Yes, you are."

"Thanks, Toots. You aren't bad either. I like a woman with a bit of meat on her bones." Colin whipped a tongue out and slathered Winifred on the chin, who squealed and giggled like a teenage girl.

Xandie's Aunt Winifred was the youngest of her supposedly late mother's sisters. Plump and of a similar short stature to Elspeth, Xandie's flighty aunt had the same amber Harrow eyes but was the complete opposite of her older sister, Amelia. Winfred was generous, cheerful, and took mothering to extreme competition levels. Her witch powers focused on spells and potions, and she made a mean candle. She had a candle, scent, and pamper store in town and was forever filling Harrow House with amazing aromas. Winifred and her daughter Holly, Xandie's other cousin, resided in Harrow House with Elspeth. Amelia and Lila chose sanity and lived in town separately.

Xandie's mother was Miranda, the eldest of the three sisters, but twenty years ago, she'd disappeared near the bluffs above Point Muse and was never seen again. Recently, there'd been some doubt cast on the presumed dead part. Enough that Xandie's late great-aunt Sera had hired a troll private investigator to dig around. And he'd found enough to know Miranda hadn't died after being chased off a cliff by a killer knight.

After being rescued by a mermaid named Coral, the trail disappeared, as did her mother. Helped along by a fanatical splinter group in the government nicknamed ASP. Anti-Species-Project. The same group that lost her mom and wasn't above blackmail to get her back. Elspeth would barely talk about her eldest daughter. Xandie was torn between wanting to find her mother and burying her head in the sand to avoid the emotional minefield her family would surely become.

Amelia closed her eyes for a second before targeting her mother with a laser stare. "You had to meddle with Mother Nature, didn't you?"

Elspeth sniffed dramatically. "I upgraded his design for optimum performance. Now he's perfect and will stand out at the pet show."

"Anyone got a smoke? I have a craving for a fat cigar." The pug waggled his eyebrows and snuggled against Elspeth's non-existent chest.

Xandie shuddered. The pug was a cigar-smoking horn-dog. The perfect match for her chaotic, eccentric, and borderline evil grandmother.

Carefully placing Colin on the ground, Elspeth

shooed him with her hand. "Do your business, Colin. No deposits on the carpet inside. We still have to discuss your costume and song choice for the talent portion of the show."

Winifred clapped in excitement. "I love the show, and now we get to enter Colin. We need to plan and talk tactics. Some of the contestants can be brutal with a new competitor." Winifred huddled with Elspeth as they whispered together.

"Is no one concerned about the cost to Colin?"

"Mom? I think the dog will survive." Lila pointed down at the aforementioned *sensitive* pug staring up her mother's skirt.

Amelia shrieked and backed away. "That animal is a menace. Let me guess, you added horny goat weed, and that caused the eruption in your spell room?"

Elspeth poked her tongue out at her eldest daughter. "I swear you take after your father with your prissy, do-no-wrong attitude, and it's my creation cave. I create life."

"That's what Dr Frankenstein said before he was attacked by a mob," Xandie whispered to her cousin.

"Xandie, your position as my favorite grand-daughter could be in jeopardy if you side with the pious naysayers."

"Never, Elspeth." Xandie distracted her grand-mother with another question. "The goat weed sparked a fire?"

"That or the noir detective novel and cigar I threw in. Who knows?" Elspeth shrugged.

Lila shook her hands in the air, exasperation clear on her face. "And the reason you made him a smoke-chugging flirt would be?"

"His manly charms and cute pug eyes will slaughter the competition." Elspeth villain chortled and then shuffled off to the house, with a still-excited Winifred in tow.

"Never you mind, Sweet Cheeks. I'll keep the dames on the straight and narrow."

"Somehow the assurance of a talking, horny pug doesn't make me feel any better." Lila grabbed Xandie and tugged her toward her bakery van. "Mom can deal with Colin and Elspeth. We need to open my shop. Business should be good with SPAFS in town."

Xandie allowed herself to be towed into the van. Lila owned and operated Heart's Delight Bakery in Point Muse. Her cousin was a Harrow witch, but all her talents lay in creating delicious baked goods that made the eater feel like they could take on the world. Except during that period a few months ago when a spate of bad luck hovered over the town and turned all her food into rotten piles of yuck. But the dastardly dragon killer had been caught, and Lila's baked goods were back to their normal delicious state.

Lila gunned the engine and swerved erratically back onto the road. Xandie buckled up tight. Unfortunately, most of the Harrow witches had a side effect of being atrocious drivers and most, including herself, didn't bother to own a vehicle. Lila and her absent cousin, Holly, had jobs that needed vehicles. Although in Holly's case, it was a fierce blue moped. And when in the mood, Elspeth delivered pizza on a hot pink, spelled moped. Lila took a corner and the van wobbled. Xandie grabbed hold of the Jesus bar. Now if she could get to the bakery in one piece, she'd be happy.

Xandie sipped her hot chocolate and sighed as its smooth, velvet goodness hit her taste buds. The pounds had crept on since she'd given up her job at Andrews College library and moved to Point Muse and her own extra special library. But hopefully walking and riding a bike everywhere would help her keep the inches off. That and giving up her yummy butter puffs. She'd weaned herself off Lila's specialty, and Xandie was now sampling different delicacies off the bakery menu every time she came in. Today's choice was a slice of supposedly healthy carrot cake.

"Worshipping at the altar of sugar again, Ms. Meyers?" Police Chief Zach Braun cocked a shaky blond eyebrow at Xandie, and the large chunk of cake paused mid shovel.

Xandie swallowed and waved her fork at the irritating, handsome shifter, who was a pain in her...

"Annoying my paying customers again, Zachy?"

"Since when does your cousin pay for her ill-gotten goodies?"

Xandie chewed slowly and then swallowed another mouthful of cake. "I'd take offense to that remark, Police Chief Braun, but in the end, it doesn't matter. I'm enjoying this cake too much." She smirked and took a sip of the liquid gold hot chocolate in her cup.

"And on that sarcastic note, I'll leave you to your sugar overdose. Stay out of trouble, ladies. The law enforcement at Point Muse would like a murder-free week for once." Braun nodded politely and ambled out.

Xandie sighed. "It's like he blames me solely for the body count in the last few months. It's the villains in town, nothing to do with me. I'm an innocent bystander."

Lila snickered. "Doesn't hurt that you're nosy. Besides, you know Elspeth thinks your Harrow witchy gift is that of a catalyst, like your mother. You make things happen. Basically, murder likes you."

Xandie wrinkled her nose. "Not something I want to advertise. Being a supernatural librarian and owner of a bad-mouthed, imp-owning black cat is enough for me."

"Theo would be enough for any sane woman." Lila bustled around wiping tables.

The SPAFS rush had eased, and the locals were poking their heads up and resuming their normal morning routines. Speaking of the pet show... Xandie turned to Lila. "Why did your mom go nuclear about Elspeth entering the pet show?"

Lila sighed and dumped her rag onto a table before collapsing into a chair next to Xandie. "Well, she's a vet and hates the idea of her mother tampering with the original nature of the animal." Lila shuddered. "Besides, that pug is slimy. That's one good reason right there."

"But she was really worked up. I wondered if

there was some kind of past issue causing her reaction."

Lila looked over her shoulder and then lowered her voice. "It wasn't always like that. Mom had a short period in her life when she couldn't get enough of the show. She trained a mini-corn and the pair dominated the show circuit."

"What's a mini-corn?"

"Miniature unicorn."

Of course. "So what happened?" Hot chocolate forgotten, Xandie leaned forward and urged Lila on.

"She became obsessed, worked Francis the mini-corn hard. He had a mental break and pooped on a judge. She was horrified and swore she'd never go near the pet show again. And she hasn't."

"And Francis?"

"He had delusions of grandeur and had Elspeth giantize him to full unicorn size. He joined a racing corn stable and broke a horn, so he had to retire. Mom never forgave herself. We never speak about it, but since SPAFS has hit town, she's on edge."

"Wow, the things you learn about your family."

Xandie marveled at the history of the Harrows. Coming from a human academic librarian background and moving into the freaky, supernatural life of the Harrows and Point Muse was certainly an education. "How does SPAFS work?"

Lila resumed wiping tables, this time next to the big picture window looking out onto Main Street. "The competitors are hard-core and take the show very seriously. Most of them are already in town, training. Elspeth will have to hurry up if she wants to enter. The welcoming ceremony is tomorrow night at Point Muse Springs Resort. It's the big opening of the resort at the same time. The pet show was supposed to be the drawcard to bring the punters."

"That's the same group from out of town who wanted to buy the land next to my Great-Aunt Sera's library?"

Lila nodded. "Yeah, they ended up buying land out of town, next to the Point Muse Academy. You know you can call it *your* library? Sera named you in her will. It's your library now, not hers."

Xandie winced. Her great-aunt Sera's murder was the first she'd had to solve in Point Muse but definitely hadn't been the last. "I know, but it feels like I'm hunting trouble if I call it mine."

Snickering, Lila peered out the window. "Trust me, you don't have to hunt trouble. It stalks you." Lila stiffened as she continued to stare outside.

"Don't tell me Elspeth's out there committing another dog atrocity against nature?" Xandie wandered over to stand next to her cousin Lila. Elspeth was nowhere to be seen. Just a group of strangers on the opposite side of the road staring down Main Street.

"Someone far worse than Elspeth," Lila hissed and quickly flipped her open sign to closed. "I'm heading to the back to do some baking. I'll reopen in an hour." Lila disappeared into the kitchen.

What zombie had gnawed on Lila's funny bone? As Xandie watched, a slim figure with short black hair detached from the group and faced the bakery, hands on hips. With a sneer and a flip of her short hair, the woman stomped off in the opposite direction.

It seemed like her mom, Elspeth, and Amelia weren't the only Harrow witches to have a mysterious past.

Xandie froze as a large black SUV with tinted windows drove down Main Street, slowing as it passed Lila's bakery. *Speaking of her mom...* That was the same kind of vehicle those idiot agents from ASP, who were hunting Miranda, liked to intimidate the common people with. She'd hoped after the gold Hesper Dragons had scared the agents in the hospital's underground parking area that ASP would steer clear.

But she guessed the lure of bait to flush out their number one enemy, Miranda Harrow, was too much to resist.

TWO

"You weren't wrong when you said the competitors take the show seriously," Xandie muttered from behind her glass of bubbly.

Lila rolled her eyes. "I told you so. Some of the popular ones come with their own entourage. Have a look." Lila pointed to a purpled-haired, wispy girl and a tall, formidable older female who stood behind her, watching.

"Who's that?"

"The emaciated purple chick is Lorelei LaRue." Elspeth sniffed. "She's won all the prelim shows and is favorite to take all round champion. Personally, her mini-corn, Fifi, is no match for my Colin."

"The other is Amity Puffin. She's the stylist and groomer for the contestants if they don't have their own. The last few prelims, she's been at LaRue's beck and call." Winifred lowered her voice. "She doesn't compete anymore and mostly runs around after Lorelei. There were rumors of a scandal when she competed years ago, but nothing concrete. The last five years, she's only groomed, not competed. Such a shame." Winifred tsked.

"Thank God Mom's not here. Seeing all these people and their enhanced animals would induce an aneurysm." Lila pointed at a flaming pink miniature unicorn prancing around Lorelei LaRue. "That's Fifi, the top contender. Mom knows the breeder who supplied LaRue with the min-corn. Fifi's from the same stable as Mom's old corn, Francis."

Winifred hushed Lila with a wagging finger and a shake of her head. "You know we don't mention that period in your mother's life."

"She isn't here. Besides, Xandie's family."

Xandie broke in before a fight erupted. "Sorry, Aunt Win. My fault. I wanted to know why Aunt Amelia was so upset at the mention of the show."

"Amelia has issues with the way some of the animals are treated while competing. Plus, she's furious at how she behaved with Francis. Her obsession got the better of her, and she can't forgive or forget."

"My daughter specializes in self-recrimination. I'm more a *get-over-it-and-what-other-kind-of-damage-can-we-do* type of person." Elspeth chugged her champagne down and waved her glass at a waiter for another. "I think it's the do-gooder genes from her father that are to blame."

Xandie had heard very little about her grandfather, Lucas Munro. Elspeth refused to talk about him except for the odd jab at his too-good nature. Amelia and Winifred both proclaimed they were too young to remember him and clammed up tight whenever his name was mentioned.

"Our elusive grandfather no one will talk about?" Xandie inquired.

"Good is like a virus, Xandie darling. Too much contact and you catch it." Elspeth shuddered dramatically before screeching as Colin raised a leg over the head of a purple, long-haired bunny rabbit. "Colin, no. Leave it until she's about to go on stage," Elspeth wailed and bolted toward the pee-challenged pug.

A tall, curvy redhead snatched the bunny up and glowered at the wrinkled grandmother. "Control your animal, madam. Princess is a gently reared sparkling Angora. I shudder to think what that nasty urine would do to her coat."

Elspeth hoisted Colin onto her hip and sneered

back. "Please, that fluffy rat looks like you dipped her in glitter before prancing out tonight. My Colin is a masterpiece."

Colin panted with his tongue out, then proceeded to lick himself. He winked at the bunny that cuddled into her owner in fright.

The woman gasped, then gagged. "You tell that oversexed monstrosity to stay away from Princess. Filthy, filthy animal." Still shuddering, the woman stomped away into the crowd.

Elspeth sniffed. "Everyone's a critic." She gently placed Colin on the ground. "We'll get her in the talent section."

"Actually, Mother, the sparkle Angora has a very good pedigree and is ranked second behind Fifi." Winifred pointed to the mini corn next to the purple-haired girl.

"Don't you listen to them. We got those others beat." Elspeth patted Colin on the head and handed him a canapé to munch on. "Filthy animal? What does that *bunny breeder* even know about the mind of my magnificent pug?" Elspeth spat out *bunny breeder* like it was a swear word.

Lila sidestepped Colin as he tried to peer up her skirt. "That's Lulu Moon. She is supposed to be an animal empath and telepath. It's a possibility she was reading Colin's mind. He's not exactly the sweetest, most innocent dog out there."

"Character. He has character," Elspeth hissed at her granddaughter. "Colin, come. We will find others who appreciate your uniqueness."

"Could you find me some red meat? I've got a powerful hankering for red meat after seeing that fluffy hors d'oeuvre." Elspeth and Colin wandered off, with Colin deviating every few paces to lift his leg.

Xandie grimaced. She could understand Amelia's freak-out over mucking with Mother Nature. It just wasn't right for a dog to talk back. She was still adjusting to Theo, her cat, and his snarky mouth, and he was an ancient Greek teenager turned into an immortal cat guardian.

"*Excuser*, Mademoiselles. Lula is not very diplomatic. She is all *temperer*." A tall, skinny man with a dominant bald spot bowed to Xandie, Winifred, and Lila.

Winifred giggled. "I have no clue what *temperer* is, but it sounds exotic."

Lila rolled her eyes at her mother's gushing. "Seriously? She has a temper, that's what he said. She gets angry."

The man nodded. "*Oui*, sadly I was married to

the harridan. Now she follows me around the show circuit to make my life a misery."

The man's fake French accent was getting on Xandie's nerves. Sprinkling in a few foreign words did not a Frenchman make.

The man bowed again to Winifred and placed a kiss on the back of her hand. "My name is Giorgio Moone. *Enchante* to meet you."

"Winifred Harrow." She gasped out her name and her cheeks pinked.

"For gawd's sakes. I think I'm going to be sick." Lila fake gagged behind Xandie's back.

"That, sadly, is my daughter, Lila. Ignore her. Our family favorite is Xandie. She's much nicer than my own offspring." Winifred beamed at Giorgio.

Lila shook again behind Xandie, her silent laughter building up into giant heaves. Xandie swallowed and then nodded to the fake Frenchman. She couldn't trust herself to speak without letting loose brays of laughter at Winifred and the fake Frenchman's antics. She had been around the Harrows for far too long. Who knew what would come out?

"George? Are you still trying to invent mystery into your life with that fake accent?" A diminutive purple-haired woman slunk up next to George and pouted. She turned and mock-whispered to

Winifred, "Don't mind old George. After he dumped poor Lulu and then she refused to take him back, all the life went out of him. Look." The girl pointed at his bald spot. "Even his hair is leaving him. So terrible." The woman made a sad face.

"Everyone needs culture in their life. Even you, LaRue." George swapped his French accent for a flat clipped tone.

"Of course they do." Patting his shoulder, she air kissed everyone, lifted her mini corn under her arm, and skipped away.

"Excuse me, please." George nodded to the women and followed behind Lorelei before grabbing her arm and dragging her off to a quieter area.

"My goodness. The blog on the Witchwebs does not do this place justice." Winifred huffed and placed her hands on her hips.

"I'm sorry, Aunt Win. I know you're a fan of the show." Xandie shoved Lila upright and at her mother. "Lila apologizes for her rude behavior too."

Caught mid-snort, Lila nodded weakly in agreement.

Winifred dropped her hands from her hips and grinned. "No apologies needed. Reality is much better. Fake Frenchman? What will they think of next?" Shaking her head, Winifred wandered off, eyes wide.

"Forget it, Xandie. Being nice in this family will get you eaten by Elspeth's cursed garden gnomes. You need to toughen up to be a Harrow." Lila slapped Xandie's back. "Speaking of our mayhem magnet grandmother, anyone wonder where she disappeared to?"

"Oh...my...God. We've lost Elspeth." Xandie glanced around, but the flagstone entertaining area out the back of Point Muse Springs Hotel and Resort was empty of the devilish, manipulative, wig-wearing elderly witch. "Is it safe to leave her by herself?"

"Safe for her or us?"

Xandie paused to think for a moment. "Both?"

"Let's split up and hunt her down. Who knows what she's up to with that unnatural dog?" Lila headed toward the makeshift stage.

Xandie decided to check out the food tents for her wayward grandmother and her obnoxious dog. Darting between bodies and dodging the odd animal, Xandie ducked inside the snack tent. Tables were full, but no Elspeth. A soothing jazz band played, and an area of grass was roped off as a small animal daycare. Anyone walking in could have mistaken the event for a normal run–of–the–mill human pet show.

Except the animals were multicolored, sometimes sparkling, and there were unicorn horns aplenty. A few even sat at tables eating with a knife and fork.

Xandie shook her head and slipped out of the tent. Thank God Point Muse was off the beaten track and settled on a clump of ley lines. Most non-humans were discouraged by the magical energy around the town and turned back before setting foot in town. The rare ones who made it through were generally already acquainted with the strange super-natural setting that was Point Muse. And Elspeth Harrow was the head priestess of weird. Not to mention the former mayor of the town, until she'd been fired for despotic behavior. Never put a semi-evil witch in charge of running a town. It never ends well.

Heated voices to the right of Xandie distracted her from Point Muse flakiness. She detoured until the voices became clearer.

"You promised me, Lorelei. Gave your word." George Moon hissed the last bit.

Xandie peered round the tent and spotted the two warring competitors, Lorelei and George. His bald spot was bright red, and the man was sweating up a swimming pool.

"Oh, Georgie. So sweet and innocent. My words

were, *I might have a line on a special tonic for that shiny bald spot*." Lorelei grabbed one of his cheeks again and gave it a sharp tug. "The line didn't pan out."

He slapped her hand away. "I left my wife for you. How could I have been so stupid? I was just a stepping stone to get you higher in the competition."

Lorelei dropped her head back and shrilled a spiteful gaggle. "You mean your introduction to the delightful Alex Pennywort, our erstwhile host? I do need to thank you for that. He's been so helpful." Lorelei smiled and stroked her lavender hair back into place.

"I want my hair tonic, Lorelei." George grabbed the woman's elbow and pulled her close. "You used me. I deserve that much from you."

Lorelei shook off George's hand and stepped away before spitting hateful words at him. "You deserve nothing. You *are* nothing but a low-level mage, and you're going nowhere, Giorgio Moone." Lorelei was still sneering as she stormed off.

"You'll give me that tonic, LaRue. If it's the last thing you ever do, you'll give me that tonic," George yelled at the purple sprite's retreating body. He glanced around self-consciously and then patted his bald spot with a handkerchief before scuttling away.

Xandie raised an eyebrow. Maybe Winifred was right to get so hooked on the show. This was like watching a soap opera unfold in person. A train wreck you couldn't stop watching.

"That purple one's devious. Her mini corn's a drama queen too. They both need an attitude adjustment, and I'm the right kind of pug to give it to them."

Speaking of train wrecks. Xandie stared down at her feet where the pug was currently raising his leg slowly.

"I have scissors, and I know how to use them. Plus, my aunt's a vet. We can do things to you you'll never fully recover from."

Colin dropped the leg. "Whoa there, bookworm. Not looking for trouble. It's instinct."

"Cock that leg at me again and we'll see where that instinct gets you," Xandie threatened the pug.

"Man, Elspeth said you girls were buzz kills."

Speaking of her meddling grandmother... "Where is Elspeth?"

Colin shifted from paw to paw. "Uh, I know nothing. Saw nothing. None of my business."

Xandie grabbed the pug before he could run and tucked him tightly under her arm. Elspeth was up to something, and she'd bet it was something to do with that stage set up out front. The woman never could resist the spotlight.

"Geez, doll-face. A healthy dose of deodorant wouldn't go astray." Colin ducked his nose away from her armpit and sneezed twice. Green boogers sprayed Xandie's arm.

Now she had a snotty, talking dog. "What else can go wrong?" Xandie appealed to the lovely blue sky overhead and then winced as Colin burped blue liquid down Xandie's leg. She should have known better than to tempt the gods and Point Muse.

Who knows what they'll throw at me next?

THREE

"Nothing to do with me." Elspeth smirked at Xandie and cooed to Colin who sat patiently at her feet.

Xandie pointed a trembling finger at the tiny brightly colored parrot burping iridescent blue bubbles. "Since I saw Colin burp up blue lemonade, I know you're the culprit. Seriously, Elspeth. You haven't even started competing yet, and you're already playing dirty."

Elspeth growled. "I didn't think it would be this boring. It's all whining about flat hair and getting some poor shmuck to fetch and carry for you." She pointed to Lorelei and the woman hovering behind her. "That purple sprite is the top competitor and as nasty as a vampire hopped up on bloodwort, and she's the most interesting thing here. I'm disillusioned."

Winifred hushed her mother. "Quiet, the host is opening the show."

Elspeth sagged in a chair and gulped a mouthful from her hip flask.

Xandie wasn't fooled. She'd found out during a stampede of walking dead party crashers at a dragon's funeral that Elspeth carried iced tea around and pretended it was Witchshine. Her grandmother liked to put on a show of chaos and mayhem, but at least some of the time, it was make-believe.

"Welcome to the annual Supernatural Pet and Familiar Show. Thanks to Point Muse Springs Resort and to the Point Muse township for a wonderful welcome." A debonair older gentleman with a pale complexion, in a snazzy black suit and red tie, swept a welcoming bow to the crowd in front of them. "I'm Alex Pennywort, host to all that is supernatural and furry. How about a big welcome to our three judges, Noble Myrddin, Velma Mystic, and Wallace Moonshadow?" The crowd responded with a dutiful clap as the judges paraded from one side of the stage to the other.

"Moonshadow?" Xandie whispered to Elspeth. The poor man looked more nervous than the competitors. Every so often, the short-statured, balding, middle-aged man would jerk uncontrollably for a few seconds. Elspeth sometimes drove Xandie to twitching, so she could sympathize with him.

"His parents were magical hippies. All about free love. They changed their last name to Moonshadow. Now their only child is an accountant and a judge at a pet show. He's a complete null. No magic gifts at all. Too much dipping into the witch herbs, I think." Elspeth raised her voice, and a woman in the front row turned and glared.

"Shush, Mother, Xandie. It's the sponsor's turn to speak now."

A large solid man stood next to the microphone, long blond curls rioting around his head like a halo and his round face gleaming. "Welcome, Point Muse residents, guests, and competitors of the Supernatural Pet and Familiar Show. I, Malachi Mede, and my wife Hannah, would like to thank you for coming to the opening of Point Muse Springs Resort." Mede waited for sporadic applause to subside. "Hannah begged me to open a resort here. As a former resident of Point Muse, she has fond memories of the town."

Lila leaned closer to Xandie. "Judging by her face, she doesn't agree. She looks like she sucked a lemon."

Xandie had to agree. Mrs. Hannah Mede did not look happy at her husband's mention of her and Point Muse.

"Kids used to tease her horribly. She was a year behind Holly and me. Her dad was human and her mom a hedge witch. She inherited the human but not the witch. Plus, she was a geeky bookworm who wore glasses. Most of the cool kids at the academy made her life hell." Lila made a face. "She was prickly too, but when she worked part-time with Mom in the vet clinic, we hung out sometimes."

"Nothing wrong with being a bookworm." Xandie ignored her cousin and focused on Hannah Mede. She might have once been a bespectacled bookworm, but those days were long ago. Curly hair cascaded down her back in a waterfall of gold. Her tight aqua dress showed not an ounce of sugar addiction. Considering Maine was tipping into fall, the poor woman had to be chilled. Maybe Mrs. Mede had come back to Point Muse to rub her superstar good looks in her ex-tormentors' faces?

Hannah sauntered over to the microphone and cooed into it, "Hello, Point Muse. Thanks for coming out to our little shindig at our new place." Hannah waved at the resort. "Isn't she pretty? So shiny and new."

Xandie had to agree with the woman. Even if there were no springs at the resort, the building more than made up for that. A mix of stone and wood, the hotel resembled an expensive mountain lodge. Gabled windows, slate gray rooms, and lovely exposed stone chimneys dotted the space. The welcoming ceremony was being held around a massive pool deck. Hannah had certainly shown her classmates she wasn't a bookworm any longer.

"As the soon-to-be premier destination of the supernatural world, I welcome you to my humble home." Hannah gestured overhead with her hands.

Xandie frowned. The banner above Hannah's head, proclaiming the resort, wavered in the wind. *Except there was no wind today.* It was a cool, calm, sunny day. The banner moved again, wavering over Mrs. Mede's head. Both sides were tied down to poles on either end of the stage, and they wavered too. One pole suddenly dipped and hit the stage. Xandie jumped up and yelled, "Duck, Mrs. Mede!"

Hannah stared nonplussed at Xandie and opened her mouth to reply but instead squealed as the banner collapsed over her and forced her to the ground. It completely covered the blonde wave of hair and half her body. Hannah Mede's skinny legs and sky-high heels stuck out.

The crowd got to their feet in a massive wave of panic. Malachi Mede and the host, Alex Pennywort, along with a tall, muscled man with a clipboard, rushed to Hannah and extricated her from her banner cocoon.

"That's a great way to make a splash back in Point Muse. Maybe the old Hannah is in there some-where after all." Lila grabbed Xandie's arm. "Let's get out of here before they blame Elspeth for the banner collapsing."

Winifred looked around. "I think that's a good idea." She hustled Elspeth and the snoring Colin away from the carnage.

Xandie followed Lila as her cousin pushed through the gaping crowd. She passed the purple-haired Lorelei LaRue, who was bending over bellowing unladylike guffaws of laughter. "Oh, that's great. Pure magic. She'll be on the Witchweb for sure. This hick town is definitely looking better."

"Lorelei! Don't let the judges hear you talking like that. They'll mark you down for sure once you start competing."

LaRue's shadow hushed her charge. "Give me a break, Amity. I have it in the bag. With Alex feeding me hints on what's up next and old Myrddin ogling me, I'm a shoo-in to win." Lorelei twitched a lock of purple hair over her shoulder. "Besides, it's not like the competition is a threat."

Wow, what a... Xandie shook her head and caught up with Lila. LaRue wasn't the nicest competitor of the bunch. She made Elspeth look like a choirgirl. *Okay, not quite, but the feeling is there.* But it sure sounded like the woman was cheating somehow. Watch out when Elspeth heard, gawd knew what her hex-loving grandmother would do about it.

"Oh, no. Seriously?" Lila moaned and jabbed Elspeth in the back. "Can't you do something about this?"

"About what?" Xandie shifted around Lila to see the cause of her cousin's emotional despair.

Elspeth growled and handed Colin off to Winifred. She hitched up her lavender pants and waded in. "It's not my fault. Damn hippie age she grew up in. They have this fake idea that all they need to do to change something is to get out with a sign. It's that free love and witch herb that ruined your mother."

"What's going on?"

Lila shoved the shorter Xandie in front of her. "If you were taller, you could block my view."

Right at the entrance to the car park, where all

the competitors and supporters were streaming in, was Aunt Amelia. Festooned with a sign covering her front and back proclaiming the evils of SPAFS, Amelia lifted her loudspeaker and screamed out a stream of catchy phrases. "Hell, no, we won't show. Hell, no. No pet show." Amelia recycled the phrases over and over. Until Elspeth took a running leap and knocked her daughter into the rose garden bordering the car park, the two women fighting for control of the loudspeaker.

Lila covered her eyes. "I can't watch this."

"Well, if it isn't Amelia *'pooping mini corn'* Harrow." Lorelei sauntered up to Lila's side and squinted at the wrestling women. A few wolf shifters with tight shirts proclaiming them to be security tried to separate the Harrow women.

"Excuse me?" Xandie frowned at the purple-haired woman next to her.

"Amelia Harrow, of the pooping mini corn fame. I thought she'd never show her face at the show again." Lorelei pouted. "But I guess memories are short. Such a shame what happened to Francis. He could have been a contender."

"Why you..." Lila's eyes bulged, and a vein throbbed in her forehead.

Pushing Lila behind her, Xandie smiled sweetly

at the mouthy woman. "Yes, that's Amelia Harrow. She'd be gratified to know she has a groupie."

LaRue spluttered, stumbling over words in order to deny her groupiness. "That's not—I mean..." Gathering her composure, she pointed as the shifter security team pulled the women apart. "How entertaining. The police have arrived now."

Police Chief Zach Braun grabbed a hissing Elspeth away as she kicked a shifter in a vulnerable spot. Xandie's grandmother had moved from dragging her daughter out of the rose bush to protecting her. Braun handed Elspeth off to his deputy sister, Melody, and plucked Amelia out of the rose bush. He forced her to sit on one side of the car park away from the fracas.

Xandie shrank back against Lila. Just what she didn't need. *Pain in her patootie Braun.* Point Muse bear shifter, police chief, and meddler in her life.

Winifred charged forward, Colin waddling at her heels. "Get it together, Mother. The judges could be watching."

Elspeth shrugged off Winifred's helping hands and dusted her pants down. "Stupid wolf shifters, need to learn to keep their paws to themselves." She shook a tiny fist at the nearest one curled up on the ground in the fetal position, whimpering. "You're lucky I'm not in my creation cave, or I'd hex you until the fleas drove you crazy."

The wolf shifter security team scuttled away from the deranged old woman as she ranted. Elspeth turned and shook an accusing finger at her protester daughter. "And you, Amelia Diana Harrow, better sleep with your eyes open. I know where you live." Elspeth gathered up a panting Colin and swept away with a babbling Winifred trailing her.

Amelia opened a bleary, bloodshot eye. "Is the mad witch gone yet?"

Zach Braun crouched next to Amelia. "Care to tell me what this is all about, Ms. Harrow?"

Amelia stood with a wince. "Crap, it's the fuzz. Take me away, copper. I got nothing to hide." Amelia extended her hands so they could be cuffed.

Braun shook his head. "Firstly, you used to change my diapers, and your mother would box my ears, and secondly, do you want to be arrested so Elspeth can't hex you?"

Amelia dropped her hands. "Maybe. Will you?"

"Not a chance. But can you tell me what this incident is all about?"

Pointing dramatically at Lorelei, Amelia raised her voice. "It's about people like her. Abusing and mistreating their pets and familiars in the name of entertainment."

"You're bitter you couldn't hack the pace of competition, old woman," Lorelei yelled back.

"Everyone knows you stack the odds, LaRue. And don't think I don't recognize Amity Puffin hanging around you like a bad smell. We all know what she really does for you." Amelia sneered.

"Please, you know nothing. You lost it when your corn pooped on a judge. Bitter old witch." Lorelei sniffed, then, turning, flounced off with her shadow, Amity, following.

"I'll stop you, Lorelei. I'll stop you from abusing your animals somehow," Amelia panted as she screeched at the purple sprite.

Braun placed a gentle hand on Amelia's shoulder and steered her toward his cruiser. "Let's have a cup of tea and a chat, okay?" He helped her into the car, and they drove out of the resort car park.

Lila massaged her forehead, then offered Xandie a weak smile. "Welcome to the real Harrow family. You sure you don't want to run screaming off into the sunset?"

Never a dull moment in a family of witches living in a freaky, supernatural, trouble magnet of a town.

FOUR

"I'd kill for a sausage, toots. How about you hop over to the big tent and fetch?" Colin gave Xandie the beady eye and scratched his tummy with a freshly trimmed rear claw.

Xandie flicked the pug on his nose. "How about I don't sic my talking cat and his pet imp on you?"

"Ew." Colin wrinkled his abused nose. "You're one of those people."

"Those people would be?"

"Cat people," Colin said, like he was talking about a murderer.

"Cat, imp, books. That's me. So, no sausage for you. Besides, the judges will be around for the appearance stage of the competition soon."

Colin puffed out his chest. "I'm magnificent.

The judges will be moved to tears." He sagged back down and squinted for a moment and then smiled.

He didn't? He wouldn't... Xandie covered her nose and gagged. *He had.*

"Better out than in, I say. How is my little man?" Elspeth cooed at Colin. She tweaked his bowtie and shifted his black velvet fedora farther forward.

"Hanging loose and low, Elspeth. How about you?"

Elspeth cackled. "Nothing a good surgeon or a nasty warlock couldn't fix. Now, are you ready to shine, my glorious pug?"

"The judges won't know what hit them."

Elspeth nodded, satisfied. She turned to Xandie. "Where's that mouthy cousin of yours?"

"Which one? I've got two to choose from." Xandie smirked. Smart mouth was a side-effect of Harrow blood.

"Since death girl is away at a dead person's conference, that would mean Lila."

Holly hated the death girl nickname Elspeth had burdened her with. She was part banshee, part witch, and worked in a mortuary, hence the nickname. Shrugging, Xandie glanced around. Little benches for both big and small animals dotted the judging room. Every competitor entered was currently giving their animals a once over before the judges came around for the first section, appearance.

"I suppose she's probably tangling with her mother. Best they're both out of the way anyway." Elspeth rubbed her hands together, then leaned conspiratorially into Xandie. "Keep an eye out for Winifred. She wouldn't approve."

Approve of what? *What fresh hell does my grandmother have planned?*

Elspeth moved toward Colin and blew a little pile of dust on him. The dust glittered purple and pink and settled over the pug in a psychedelic cloud.

Colin coughed and snorted. His little fedora hat flew through the air when a huge sneeze erupted from his hairy muzzle. Green and purple colored snot spattered Xandie, Elspeth, and the nearest competitor, Lorelei LaRue.

"Harrows," Lorelei squealed and tried to flick the substance off her gauzy cream tea dress. "You're all a menace."

Xandie grimaced and used Colin's hat to wipe the mess off the hysterical woman. "Sorry, Colin has allergies."

Lorelei hissed at Xandie. "That oversexed hairy furball will never win. My Fifi has more breeding in her little horn then he does in all of his neck rolls."

Elspeth bared her teeth and covered Colin's ears. "Ignore her. She needs a good feed of red meat. She's lacking iron." Elspeth narrowed her eyes. "Or she will be when I'm done with her."

"Yeah, that mini corn. *Whoa, what a dame.*" Colin winked at the mini corn currently cowering next to Amity Puffin, hairstylist of the competition.

"You leave Fifi alone, you Harrow-made menace," Lorelei screeched and planted herself in front of her stylist.

Xandie intervened. "I'm sure Colin and Elspeth didn't mean to hurt you or insult Fifi. Let's all calm down before the judges arrive." Xandie faked a smile and nodded at Amity. "Are you here to prepare Fifi? I thought I saw a smudge on her coat."

Both women squealed and immediately lost interest in Elspeth, fawning over the mini corn instead.

"Elspeth, keep your cool. That purple woman is obsessed. You never know what you might find on your doorstep if she loses it."

"I'd like to see her try, Xandie. I have the most perfect hex for her and that Fifi. Anyone spell *hair and fur loss*?" Elspeth spat her words out, outrage obvious in every bone in her body.

"Mother. What have you done?" Winifred stood,

arms crossed, glaring at Colin. Or at the glittery purple patches that now covered his back.

"Yeah, I got a powerful itch. Anyone got a back scratcher?" Colin raised a leg and scratched furiously toward his back.

"No!" Elspeth wailed. "He was supposed to sparkle, not itch."

Xandie poked one of the patches of purple. "Looks like an allergic reaction. Maybe you should get Amelia to have a look?"

Winifred and Elspeth grimaced as one. "Not a good idea and we can't throw another spell at him. It could make his reaction worse."

"Oh dear. That doesn't look good." The tall man with the clipboard who'd run to Hannah Mede's rescue when the banner collapsed, stood next to them.

"My poor baby." Elspeth sobbed crocodile tears over Colin's patchy purple coat.

"We're due to start in ten minutes. You need to find something to clear it up or cover his coat. Otherwise, the other competitors will eat him alive."

Xandie narrowed suspicious eyes at the man standing next to Colin. He towered over her and had a swarthy olive complexion with curly dark brown hair. With heavily muscled shoulders and arms, he didn't exactly look like the pet show type. "And you are?"

The man snapped to attention and saluted with his clipboard. "Davros Mazani, at your service. I'm the producer and head ringleader for this circus."

Elspeth lifted her head, and the tears magically disappeared. "You related to Olga Mazani?"

"My dearly departed, sainted grandmother."

"She cheated at poker."

He shrugged. "A saint's gotta win a round or two of poker sometimes." He checked his watch. "You don't have much longer to find something to help the purple monster."

Winifred snapped her fingers. "Quick, Xandie, head to the food tent. Some baking soda and warm water might help."

Xandie nodded and took off at a run. The quicker she was, the less time Elspeth had to set off witch world war three with the not-so-nice Lorelei LaRue. Taking a shortcut behind the judging team, Xandie yelped as she ran into two well-dressed men, whispering animatedly. Xandie hit the grass with a thump. Thankfully, her rear end was well padded, courtesy of Lila's baking.

One of the men, a solid built blond, Malachi Mede, offered a hand to Xandie. "Sorry, Miss..." He hauled Xandie to her feet and stared quizzically at her.

Blushing at her clumsiness, Xandie offered an apologetic smile. "Meyers. Xandie Meyers. We've got a bit of a rash problem and judging is soon. I should have looked where I was going."

The other gentleman, this one with almond-shaped eyes and close-cropped black hair, bowed to Xandie. "Apologies, Ms. Meyers. I thought I'd offer my salutations to Mr. Mede on the opening of his lovely resort. Unfortunately, we chose an inappropriate spot." He bowed again. "Malachi, I look forward to speaking about the resort another time." He nodded to Xandie and quickly left.

Someone is eager to leave? But was it because of her clumsiness or something else? Switching on the charm, Xandie offered her own apologies. "Sorry for disturbing your chat. I didn't think anyone was behind the judging tent right now."

Malachi Mede looked uncomfortable for a moment but recovered swiftly. "No worries, Ms. Meyers. Rashes are more important than listening to someone gush over your place. Please excuse me, I have to find my wife. She's overseeing the food for tonight's cocktail party." Mede nodded and disappeared into his resort.

Something made her think his meeting had been a tad more important than gushing over the resort or gossiping about the health conditions of the pet show contestants...*Colin*. Xandie took off again, this time for the food tent.

Pushing open the flap, Xandie waited for a moment to let her eyes adjust to the absence of glare. The beginning of fall in Maine was glorious, and Point Muse had turned on its welcoming weather for the pet show. But it made it hard for a girl to see what condiments she needed for an Elspeth-caused rash.

"Lunch isn't until one." A woman in a chef's smock glared at Xandie.

The same dark-haired woman who'd sneered at Lila's bakery the other day. The same person Lila had run away from and then procasti-baked for hours.

"I need some baking soda for a rash emergency." Xandie crossed her fingers that the woman could help, otherwise she'd have to test her lungs and legs and search out the resort kitchen double time.

The chef frowned. "I think I have some in the kitchen." She pointed a red-tipped finger at Xandie. "Stay there." She disappeared into the back of the tent.

Xandie tapped her fingernails on the benchtop

and snuck a look at the food in the glass cabinets. Only a few dishes were out, but everything looked delicious. One thing could be said for Malachi Mede. He'd spared no expense in opening his resort and hosting the pet show.

"Here." The chef shoved a small box at Xandie. "Bring it back if there's anything left. God knows the last thing I need is someone accusing me of stealing product."

"Nothing new for you, Madelyn. Being accused of stealing, I mean," Lila growled from behind Xandie.

"I did not steal your recipe, Harrow. We happened to submit the same recipe at the same time. You're sore because you lost your place. Only the best is offered a place at the Witchbonne." The chef smirked.

Xandie juggled her box of baking soda and stepped out of the firing zone.

"You mean the crookedest. The only way you got in was by cheating and stealing my flambé." Lila stood with her fingers curled into fists, sparks shooting from her clenched fingers...literal sparks.

"Well, you almost ruined my dish. That means you cheated too."

Lila drew back. "Liar."

"You set my flambé on fire."

"It's supposed to be on fire."

"Not when a judge is eating it. You're lucky they saw the funny side and scored me for creativity." The chef bared her teeth in a shark smile. "In fact, you could say you helped me into that position all by your witchy old self."

Lila raised her fist into the air. "You'll get yours, Madelyn Luna. Karma loves a cheater." Lila grabbed Xandie's arm and towed her out of the tent.

"Not a friend then?" Xandie quirked an eyebrow in question.

Lila released her grip on Xandie's arm and took a deep breath. "Sorry, she's a sore spot with me. Luna stole one of my recipes and used it to get into one of the best witch cooking schools we have. I can't stand her."

"That's the woman you saw yesterday outside the bakery?"

"Yeah, I try to avoid her. She brings out the witch in me." Lila offered a shamefaced smile to Xandie.

"Well, if I don't get this to Elspeth..." Xandie held up the baking soda, "then we'll both be seeing the witch in Elspeth."

"Lead on, scaredy-pants Meyers. God forbid you tangle with a geriatric witch." Lila bowed.

"Have you met our grandmother? She'd scare an angel into retreating."

"True." Lila took off running.

Jogging to the judging tent, Xandie burst in with a huff and made a beeline to her grandmother and Aunt Winifred.

"Sorry it took so long. Lila was about to have a fight with the caterer." Xandie extended the box to her grandmother. Both women stood on tiptoes, whispering to each other. Davros, the producer, had disappeared.

"Is this some Harrow bonding thing I don't know about?" Xandie murmured to Lila, who shrugged.

"Who knows with those two?"

"Shush. We're trying to listen." Winifred hushed her nieces.

Xandie shot Lila a confused glance and dumped the baking soda box next to a snoring, purple-patch-covered Colin. "Let's get closer and have a look." Xandie pushed through the crowd of competitors and onlookers. A thin wail echoed over the crowd's rising noise.

"Over there." Lila pointed to the curtained-off grooming section, where three judges currently lingered.

Lila shifted in front of the curtain to sneak a peek. A female loudly sobbed from behind.

"What's going on?" Xandie asked a little man with a frizzed-out mop of a bird sitting on his shoulder.

"Murder." He drew the word out with relish.

Another one? Maybe she *was* a body magnet? Elspeth and Winifred were fine, who could it be? "Who was killed?"

"That purple be-witch Lorelei and her mini corn. Might open the field up to the rest of us." The little man smiled with a mouthful of teeth filed to points.

"Xandie, look." Lila pointed to the curtain, as it twitched back to reveal Chief Zach Braun, a sobbing Amity Puffin, and an angry Amelia Harrow.

But that wasn't the only thing it revealed. Standing still as a statue behind Amelia with hands in the air was a petrified Lorelei LaRue and her mini corn, Fifi.

Zach Braun turned toward Amelia. "I'm sorry, Ms. Harrow. But I need to ask you a few questions down at the station." With that, he led her away from the tent, along with Amity.

Here we go again. Xandie Meyers, dead body magnet, back in business.

FIVE

"Can't believe that obnoxious glittering rabbit took first place in appearance." Elspeth limped around the room with her arm in a sling.

Lila snickered while she dusted her cousin's kitchen bench. "I can't believe you hexed the golden goose to lay an egg on its head."

Elspeth growled. "I was trying to smother the damn rabbit with the goose. How was I to know their owners used to be married and the animals had grown up together?"

"How about you try not to kill your competitors? Might help." Xandie shuddered, the chaos at the appearance judging stage was not something she was likely to forget. After the police had carefully removed Lorelei, the judges had continued with their rounds and awarded best place to Lulu Moon's glitter Angora rabbit. Elspeth had not dealt with defeat well.

"I *see* you, Alexandra. Your position as my favorite granddaughter is tenuous at best."

"God's sake, Gran. You lost. Give it up."

Elspeth pointed her finger at Lila. "I was robbed." She sighed. "Fine, maybe getting Colin to belch radioactive gas on that phoenix was a bit much, but how did I know she'd go up in flames and set the tent on fire?" Elspeth pointed at her sling-bound arm. "I was injured too. Didn't do that on purpose."

Xandie coughed into her hand and ignored Elspeth's dramatics. She'd rather hear from Lila. "Have you heard anything about your mom?"

Lila dropped her cloth and leaned against the kitchen bench that was now covered in an overdose of baking goods. "Nothing since the last update. They interviewed her all night about Lorelei and their history together. Winifred left a little while ago to try to break her out of the station."

"And release her I did, my darlings." Winifred stood in the doorway of the kitchen, dragging an obviously weary Amelia with her.

"Mom." Lila rushed to give her a quick, hard hug

before glaring at her. "You'd better tell us everything, or we're setting Elspeth on you."

Amelia sagged into her chair. "Winifred filled me in on the antics. Why am I not surprised? That damn show always brings out the worst in people."

"What happened, Aunt Amelia?"

"The same thing that happens to every Harrow witch. Bad timing." Amelia stared off into space for a moment. "I went in to have a chat with Amity Puffin. I wanted to make sure she wasn't up to her old tricks of supplying unnecessary cosmetic potions to the competitors. But I couldn't find her. Decided to check in her grooming area. Walked in and found Lorelei and Fifi petrified. That's when Amity found me. She called Braun in, and the rest you saw." Amelia grimaced. "I hated LaRue and what she was doing to poor Fifi. But I'd never hurt them. Besides, how can I turn anyone to stone? I'm an animal lover, not a killer."

Who or what stoned Lorelei then? "Do the police have any ideas yet?"

"Zach wouldn't let anything slip, but Aggie told me they ruled out spells or potions after testing a stone sliver of Lorelei's hair. About the only other thing that could do that naturally is a basilisk or a gorgon."

"And for the newly supernatural among us?" Xandie would head into the library once the others left and dig out more information, but for now, a quick download of basic info would do.

"A basilisk is a reptile hatched from a cock's egg and can turn anyone to stone with their stare. A gorgon is a woman with snakes for hair who can also turn someone to stone," Elspeth announced with a wave of her uninjured hand. "Malachi Mede's the only Medusa descendant, but he's male and can't inherit any of the gifts."

Only in Point Muse. "What about a basilisk then?"

"A basilisk's a high-level, dangerous breed and has to be licensed with the local vet and council. Mom would have said if there was anyone in town with a basilisk." Lila dumped a mug of herbal tea in front of her mother. "Drink up. You need energy and a calming influence."

Amelia took a gulp of tea and hissed as the bitter herbs hit the back of her throat. "There are no basilisks in town right now, but I have treated one in the last six months. I'm assuming as the police are currently searching my vet practice, they'll find my treatment records."

"Plus, we have a bigger problem than that."

Elspeth paused dramatically. "They have banned me from competing." She looked around expectantly. "Well? Where is your outrage? I expected more from my family." Elspeth covered a snoring Colin's ears. "It's all right, my poor rejected pug. Mommy still loves you."

As one, the Harrow witches gagged. Seeing her sometimes hex-loving grandmother coo over an over-sexed, wrinkled pug scared Xandie.

"Haven't you lot left yet?" Theo, Xandie's talking black cat, wandered in with his pet imp Horatio doing handstands on his back.

"Can't block greatness, evil feline." Colin sneezed on Elspeth, then gave the imp a beady eye. "No one ever told you that you shouldn't play with your food?"

Theo hissed and swerved to stand next to Xandie, then sighed. "Are you going to allow that manufactured monstrosity to insult Horatio like that?"

Dramatic animals, the lot of them. Xandie held up her hand in a timeout signal. "Cease and desist with the insults. We're here to make sure Aunt Amelia's all right."

"And to make sure she stays out of jail," Lila

added. "Considering she's a Harrow, that could be difficult."

"I'm sitting right here, daughter." Amelia sighed. "But sadly, I agree with you. To the police, it probably looks like an open and shut case."

"But not to Xandie. She's a detective extraordinaire. She has to stumble across another body sooner rather than later. That will get you off the hook." Lila looked hopefully at Xandie.

"No, no, no. We have to look at the most serious problem we have right now." Elspeth chugged a gulp from her hip flask.

"Who killed Lorelei?" Amelia offered.

"Who's targeting Aunt Amelia?"

"Why is Colin belching yellow clouds of gas?" Winifred battered at a hazy cloud in front of her and moved to the opposite side of the kitchen.

"Why hasn't some foreign country arrested Elspeth yet?" Lila sneered at her grandmother.

"Ingrates, the lot of you. I was speaking of the issue of Colin competing."

Lila whispered to Xandie, "If she's banned, we have a way out of that furry horror show, don't we?"

"We need someone to compete with Colin if Elspeth can't."

Everyone stared at Amelia, shocked to hear that come out of her mouth.

Elspeth recovered first and eyed Amelia suspiciously. "Who are you, and what have you done with my daughter?"

"Your craziness finally drove me to it." Amelia smiled, then sobered. "I don't want to go to jail. We need someone on the inside. They won't let Theo enter his imp, and the rest of us don't have animals. Elspeth is banned. We only have Colin now."

Everyone swiveled to stare at Xandie. *No way.* Not another dead body investigation. "No. Let Braun handle the case. He'll see sense about Amelia's involvement."

Theo coughed a fur ball onto Xandie's feet. "Please, we all know you'll cave. You're a Harrow groupie."

Horatio the imp cheered wildly and poked a finger in Theo's eye.

Yowling, Theo blinked rapidly and bucked Horatio to the floor. The imp shook a fist at Theo and scampered out the kitchen door, heading for Xandie's library.

"As my oh-so-noisy pet pointed out, viciously, to me, it's not my choice, and Xandie does have a gift for the macabre. Maybe she *should* investigate. But I make no promises about fur balls and your walk-in closet." Theo followed the imp out the door.

Elspeth wiggled in excitement. "That's decided then. Xandie will show Colin, and Winifred can coach her. Watch out, competition, the Harrows are back." She coughed into her hand. "And we'll clear my daughter's name, of course. First priority...well, maybe second. But we'll do it." Elspeth collared Winifred and consulted in a secretive planning session with her daughter.

"When did I get railroaded into this?"

Snickering, Lila slapped Xandie on the back. "When you came to town and found out you had Harrow blood, *sucker*." Lila led Amelia out of the kitchen. "I'm taking Mom home for a shower. Winifred can take Elspeth and Colin home."

"So, it's just you and me, kid. A match made in a Harrow cauldron. The two of us taking on SPAFS together." Colin winked at Xandie and belched another radioactive cloud into the kitchen. "Man, that burrito Elspeth doctored with pixie dust is a killer on my indigestion." Colin rubbed his tummy with a grimace.

On that note...

"Right, Aunt Win? Take Elspeth and Colin home for now. I'll consult with the library and meet up tomorrow before the next event." Xandie pushed Winifred and Elspeth out her kitchen door.

Winifred snatched a grumbling Colin on the way and shooed her mother out.

Elspeth yelled over her shoulder, "Don't you worry, Xandie. We'll plan everything. You'll be a competing machine when we finish with you."

Xandie groaned and hurried into the library. Who knew what fresh hell Elspeth had planned for her now?

"I guess you agreed then?" Theo perched on the top of a shelf of scrolls, cleaning his imp-free fur.

Xandie grabbed a couple of books and shelved them. "Looks like. It'll be fine. I just have to deal with that egomaniac, Colin."

"And dodge a killer and dead bodies."

"Hey, it's only Lorelei and Fifi so far. I'm sure Chief Braun can handle it. I'll be fine."

Theo stopped his grooming and leaped onto the library desk. "I hope so. It'd be a pain in my furry rear end to have to break in another one of you librarians."

The library's lights flickered overhead. Normally, Xandie wore a gold necklace with a triangle symbol with an engraved open eye. It was her link to the library. But she found out when she tangled with a killer knight that she didn't actually need to use it to communicate with the sentient library. The Great Library of Alexandria had purposely let its physical building burn during ancient Greek times so it could protect all supernatural knowledge.

Since the eighteen hundreds, the library had rested in Point Muse, Maine, a supernatural town anchored around a hub of ley lines. After its destruction, the library was always paired with a librarian and the super grouchy, Theophilous, a.k.a. Theo, a talking black cat who'd been caught in the original fire and turned from a scroll-porn-reading, hip-flask-drinking ancient Greek teenager into a cat guardian.

Xandie's great-aunt Sera had been the previous librarian, until she'd been killed. Xandie's mother, Miranda, had brought Xandie down to Point Muse and Aunt Sera every vacation to spend time with her. Now she wondered if that had been to get her used to the library and being the librarian. Sera had been her father's aunt, but he couldn't stand her or Point Muse. After Miranda had disappeared, he washed his hands of Point Muse. Xandie had only phone and email contact with Sera after that. Until she died and Xandie inherited the library and Theo.

She rubbed a hand along the desk to soothe the

library. "It's all good, I promise. How bad could a supernatural pet show be?" Xandie grabbed a few requests for library help and wrote them into the appointment book. Both inscriptions dissolved and reappeared on different dates. The library decided who had access to her and what information was supplied. She'd been quiet of late, refusing visitors, so it was good to see the old girl opening her doors again.

"Did you ask the library what's going on?" Theo placed his paw on the open appointment book.

Since SPAFS was a supernatural pet show, odds were, it wasn't a human killing so the library might have some information. For once, Theo had a good idea.

Xandie glanced around the room. Horatio the imp was curled up on Theo's cushion snoring, but the rest of the room was quiet. Beautiful wooden shelving around the room covered in books and scrolls, and polished reading tables and chairs, sat tidily together. No stray books out of place and no mischievous scrolls dueling each other. Why did she feel it was the calm before the storm? "Library? What supernatural creature turned Lorelei and Fifi into stone?"

A wooden bookcase next to the photocopying

room wiggled for a moment. Then a small, gilt-edged, blue-covered book flew into Xandie's hand, and she smiled her thanks. Opening the book with care, she settled onto a couch. *"Basilisk Care: How Not to End Up as a Garden Ornament."* Xandie read the title out loud. Catchy, but not exactly market friendly.

She continued, "Basilisks are purported to be serpent kings hatched from a cock's egg and can turn one to stone with a single glance. Can range in size from twelve fingers in length to the size of a large dog. On their heads, they have a crown-shaped crest. They have a bird-shaped face, with dragon wings and a serpent tail. They walks upright on bird legs and their putrid breath can wither plants." Xandie shuddered. "So can Colin's." She didn't know who'd be worse, a basilisk with a stony gaze or an enchanted pug with a toxic butt.

"Best thing anyone can do is to avoid a basilisk. But it does have a weakness and is terrified by weasels. Weasels are also immune to a basilisk's glare or bite. If in the vicinity of a basilisk, a mirror is a worthy defense as well. The basilisk is not immune to its own gaze, and if using a mirror back at it, the animal can be turned to stone. The basilisk is classified as a high-level dangerous breed and must be registered with the local vet and all supernatural councils. Basilisks are deemed controllable by the use of an amulet, but the making and use of said amulet is highly regulated."

What's the bet Elspeth had some knowledge of basilisk control amulets with her underhanded dealings on the witch black-market? The couch Xandie was currently curled up on quivered as she finished reading. Xandie placed the book down on a side table and rubbed the wood of the table softly, trying to settle the library. With Sera dying, her mother going missing, and having to help save Xandie from a killer knight, the poor old library had attachment issues.

"It's all good. I promise you; I'll be fine tomorrow."

How bad could a supernatural pet show really be?

SIX

"I promise all competitors that any hoof and horn disease carriers have been quarantined this morning. There's no cause for alarm. Everything has been dealt with." Hannah Mede tried to smile, but the raised green blisters on one side of her face forced a grimace instead. "The competition is perfectly safe."

Lila leaned into Xandie. "Except for all those diseased mini corns running around. I mean, look at her face."

Hannah glowered at Lila and Xandie. "But for those who *are* worried about contamination, the blisters on my face are caused by an allergy to mugwort. There's no reason to be alarmed. The chef is preparing an amazing feast for a sit-down lunch today. So, thank you for coming and please, enjoy yourselves." Hannah stepped down from the small podium and had a hurried conversation with Madelyn Luna and the producer before the chef and Davros hustled off.

Time to start investigating. Xandie made a beeline for Hannah. "Mrs. Mede? I wanted to thank you for the opportunity to compete in place of my grandmother, Elspeth Harrow. It means a lot."

Hannah smiled lopsidedly at Xandie. "The Harrows have been around Point Muse since the town formed. Wouldn't seem right if they were excluded."

"Your family has been here a long time too, Hannah." Lila popped up next to Hannah and gave her a quick hug.

Hannah stood stiff as a board before sagging slightly and giving Lila a quick squeeze in return. "Hey, Lila. How are you?"

Lila stepped back and shrugged. "As good as can be expected between Elspeth and my mother's antics."

Hannah checked around to make sure they were alone. "I don't know what's going on, but Amelia would never hurt Fifi. That horrible Lorelei maybe, but not the animal.

Xandie introduced herself. "I'm Lila's cousin,

Xandie Meyers." She shook Hannah's hand and got down to business. "We're positive someone framed Amelia. We just don't know who."

"It's this damn pet show. I swear it's cursed. Ever since I came back to Point Muse, things have been going wrong."

Lila frowned. "What do you mean? What things?"

Hannah grabbed a long curly blonde lock and twiddled the end. "That banner collapsing, my face allergy, power off and on at the resort. Some of my clothing missing and then having to deal with that woman, Lorelei. She was horrible. She even demanded an extra dressing room at the resort. But I guess I didn't want her and Fifi to die." Hannah lowered her voice. "We found a chimera statue first thing this morning. No sign of his owner. It's like he vanished. And I swear someone keeps following me. This nasty short man with a yellow-gray beard. I see him everywhere."

What were the odds these were all coincidences? Xandie had a question. "Lorelei had another dressing room? I thought all the competitors were given areas to use as their own in the one tent."

"Usually, but somehow, she got my husband to give her space at the resort. Not a real room, of course. It's a small office Malachi turned into a dressing room for her. It's off the resort kitchen. I have no clue why he'd do that for such a horrible woman. But they were always having meetings behind closed doors. I..." Hannah stopped, her cheeks pink. "I thought they were having an affair, but it was pretty obvious my husband couldn't stand her. I don't know why he spent so much time with her."

The police had searched the tent changing rooms already, but they might not have known about the extra dressing room. Xandie focused on Hannah. "How long have you been married to Mr. Mede?" Xandie hoped Hannah wouldn't clam up if Lila was here. Because Hannah might be on to something. Why would a rich, happily married Malachi Mede hand out special favors to a nasty piece of work like LaRue?

Hannah smiled. "I'm Malachi's second wife. His first love divorced him years ago for a centaur. We've been married for a little over two years now. He's sweet, treats me like a pampered princess."

Lila cocked her head and considered her old friend. "Is that enough for you? I mean no offense, but you were pretty smart at school. Mom expected you to go into medicine or science. Not be a..."

"A trophy wife?" Hannah grimaced. "I found out quickly that most supernatural men aren't after brains. Then my parents died, and Malachi came along. I guess I fell into line with the blonde bombshell image." Hannah whipped out a book on Nicola Tesla's inventions from her handbag. "But you can't take the book out of the girl, I guess."

"And you decided to build a resort here in Point Muse?" Xandie guessed Hannah wanted to show her bullying classmates how far she'd come.

"I started getting homesick. Not everywhere is like Point Muse. I begged Malachi to build here. Originally, he said no, it would be too expensive, but he eventually came around." Hannah scowled. "I wish he hadn't come up with the pet show angle for the launch. It's been horribly tense since they showed up. Malachi's always in a meeting with that Japanese man. He's in hotels too, but I guess a businessman has to do whatever they need to in order to close a deal." She checked her watch. "Sorry to gossip and run, but I need to make sure that nasty chef is running on time for lunch." Hannah waved goodbye and trotted off in her ridiculously high heels.

Lila yelled out to Hannah, "Watch out for that chef! She's bad news."

"Give it a rest, Lila. We have more important issues to focus on than a food feud."

"What's more important than ruining Madelyn Luna's reputation?" Lila stood with her hands on her hips.

Xandie ticked points off on her fingers. "Find out who killed Lorelei, Fifi, and the chimera. Find out who's framing your mother, and search LaRue's secret dressing room before Braun does. Work out why there are so many accidents happening around Hannah and the resort, find out who's following her, and control Elspeth's cheating manipulative ways." Xandie groaned at the large list of mystery to-dos.

Lila bopped Xandie on the nose. "You forgot one."

"What?"

"Win the pet show so Elspeth doesn't curse you for the rest of your tragically shortened life." She smiled widely and winked.

"Thanks, cousin. You're a gem." Xandie stomped off in search of Winifred and the disaster in the making, Colin the show pug. She ignored Lila's smirk. Honestly, some days, you just had to ignore your family and get on with sleuthing.

In the end, finding Winifred was easy. Colin, on the other hand, was a little harder.

"Where is he, Aunt Winifred?" Xandie tapped her foot and glared at her normally beaming aunt.

Winifred wrung her hands. "I swear, he was here complaining about the doggy yoga I had him doing. He's coming off cigar withdrawal and is so grumpy. I thought the yoga would relax him. I grabbed him a toy cat to chew on, and then he disappeared. Mother's going to hex me when she finds out."

"Not if we find him first." Odds were Elspeth was already involved in Colin's disappearance. Her maniacal grandmother probably had some devious and underhanded plan in play involving the pug. Xandie glanced around. No one was screaming at the dirty dog's antics, so the dressing tent was clear. "Stay here, and stall if anyone asks about Colin." She patted her aunt on the arm and ducked outside.

"Where on earth are you, Colin?" Xandie stopped in the middle of the flagstone walkway and considered her options. There were three things Colin cared about. Cigars, food, and females. No way would anyone sell cigars to a pug.

That left food and females.

The back of Xandie's neck itched. Rubbing the skin, she turned. No one was nearby, but still her skin prickled. There'd been a few times in the last week her skin had crawled like a thousand eyes were watching...or maybe a few of those ASP morons. Shaking the feeling, Xandie sped off toward the food tent and Lila's nemesis, Chef Madelyn Luna.

Lifting the tent flap, Xandie cautiously peered in. A few people having coffee nodded their heads hello, but otherwise, everything seemed calm and Colin-free.

"In or out but stop propping open the tent flap," Chef Luna snapped at Xandie.

Into the lion's den... Xandie slipped in and forced a smile. "Sorry, I'm currently hunting a talking pug called Colin. Have you seen him at all? He has an obsession with red meat."

"*You*," Madelyn hissed and grabbed Xandie by the arm, towing her into a curtained-off kitchen preparation area. "*That.* That's what happened." She pointed to the pots and pans littering the floor, along with empty meat packets. "I had fifty packets of hamburger meat. Now I have none. Your lousy pug was the four-legged culprit."

Lila would either blow her top or revel in Madelyn's anguish. Either way, it would be another Harrow drama. *Time for damage control.* "Can you conclusively prove that it was Colin the pug? That's a lot of meat for one little dog."

"Three things. A big puddle of purple-colored

pee, a dog's paw print, and I saw his flabby butt high-tailing it out of here. He yelled I was a grumpy dame who needed to eat more." Madelyn scowled at Xandie. "How are you going to fix this?"

Oh, Colin. If you do the crime, don't get caught. Elspeth's first rule of dirty deeds. "Bill Harrow House for the meat and fix something else for lunch. Aren't you meant to be a renowned Witchbonne chef?" *Zinger, baby.*

Madelyn growled. "Whatever. Like I said, trust you Harrows to be involved in mayhem." She held up a hand to forestall Xandie's words. "I don't care if you're a Meyers, you've still got Harrow blood. Nosy mayhem magnets, all of you. Look at the trouble going on at the show right now."

Xandie protested, even though she couldn't help agreeing with the chef's words. "We didn't murder anyone here. Bodies just seem drawn to us for some reason. It's not our fault."

Scoffing at her words, Madelyn collected the meat wrappers and shoved them into the trash can. "I suppose that could happen, but still, this place and you Harrows are cursed. Trouble follows you."

Madelyn was always around the pet show people, so maybe she'd heard something? "Can't blame you there. Harrows' middle name is chaos.

But we aren't the culprits this time. Have you seen anything strange or suspicious while you've been working here?"

"In Point Muse, everything is strange, but this resort takes the witch prize for wacky. The power's always surging here, and accidents keep happening when the owner, Hannah Mede, is around. Food spoiling, allergic reactions, furniture breaking, clothing missing. You name it. Don't get me started on the freaks hanging around her either." Madelyn grabbed a handful of pots and stowed them away, out of sight.

Talk about way too many coincidences featuring Hannah Mede. But was it her the killer was after or something to do with the resort? "What freaks are we talking about exactly? Point Muse ones or the psycho killer kind?"

"Who knows in this place? But the creep looked dirty and unkempt. A short, older guy with a yellow-stained beard. He's always following her, but I've seen him talking to Mr. Mede and that polite Japanese guy, Mr. Shan. Now could I have some peace to get some cleaning done?"

"Sorry again for the mess." Xandie paused at the kitchen exit. "Any idea where the pug was headed?"

"Last time I saw his flabby behind he was heading toward the resort kitchen."

Xandie waved thanks as Madelyn yelled at her again, "My invoice for the meat will be in the mail this afternoon."

"Damn you, Colin. Couldn't keep your nasty paws off the food?" Speaking of food, she needed to get up to the kitchen pronto. Before he did more damage they couldn't afford.

Xandie reached the kitchen and the open back door. *This doesn't bode well.* The same back door where an annoyed Hannah Mede's voice was currently floating out. "Don't blame the dog. The door was left open. That's a health and safety issue, not an animal control one."

Xandie poked her head in the doorway. A group of white-shirted kitchen attendants grouped around Hannah, wiping her down with towels. Milk and eggs, mixed together in a dairy and shell minefield, covered the floor. Colin had obviously visited the kitchen for a drink after his red meat feast. "Hannah? Are you okay?"

Hannah pulled a towel off her matted blonde ringlets. "Hi, Xandie. I guess you're looking for a runaway pug?"

Xandie grimaced. "I'm sorry. He's Elspeth's dog, and he has a mind and a voice of his own."

Hannah giggled. "I guessed that when he told me I had nice gams. Then I slipped in a puddle of milk and got covered in this mess. He took off before I could grab him."

Snatching a cloth, Xandie rubbed at a massive piece of shell attached to Hannah's back. "I'm sorry about this. I hope you're okay."

Hannah waved off the kitchen staff and motioned for Xandie to follow her. "Don't apologize. At least this accident I can blame on a talking dog. It's all the bad luck that's happening to me that I can't explain that freaks me out." Hannah grabbed a clean towel from a bench in front of a bank of lockers and swiped at her shirt. "And I'm not crossing Elspeth Harrow for anyone. Colin gets a free pass."

After dumping the egg-covered towel into a laundry bag, she considered Xandie for a moment and then leaned against the lockers. "Now if someone was interested in solving Lorelei LaRue's murder, and they stepped through the unlocked door over there to the left, they might be able to have a sneak peek at LaRue's second dressing room before the police arrived." Hannah winked and sashayed off.

"Hannah Mede, you are full of surprises." Xandie checked her surroundings, then pushed the door open to Lorelei's secret room. It was only a small office, but Lorelei had managed to turn all available space into a dumping ground for everything purple in the world. A small window, decorated with a purple and silver gauzy curtain, looked out toward the staff car park. A metal folding desk and matching chair had been shoved up into the corner and stacked high with an extensive collection of expensive makeup. Clothing lay in piles on the floor and draped over a small sofa.

Xandie picked through the pigsty and was struck by a severe case of déjà vu. She felt like she'd been in this position before, searching through someone's life garbage. At least that strange feeling of being watched had disappeared. For now. Hopefully, those ASP agents after her supposedly disappeared mother had given up.

Xandie shoved clothing around the floor with her foot. All she learned was that Lorelei had been a disorganized piglet. She shuddered at the thought of what Theo would do to a pile of her clothing. He was annoyed enough she was undercover at the same show that refused to let him compete with his own imp.

Shifting aside a pile of sparkly purple mini corn collars, Xandie uncovered a small framed photo. It was a shot taken of Lorelei, draped over a purple racing corn's neck. She stood in front of a racetrack, grinning widely at the camera and holding a trophy aloft. And there in the background was a short old man with a yellow beard, along with a disgruntled-looking Malachi Mede.

"Interesting." Could that be the grimy man following Hannah, the one Madelyn Luna described? "How are you connected to Lorelei?" Xandie tapped the photo with a nail, and a small yellow ticket slipped out from the frame.

Frowning, Xandie picked it up and studied the ticket. Most of the writing on the slip read like a foreign language. *Race eleven. Acacia cup. Illusion Park* stood out. Illusion Park was home to the racing corns, the same animal that Lorelei was hanging off in the photo. Was the grimy bearded old man some kind of bookie? Lorelei obviously loved the racing corns, but was she an owner or a gambler? What was the connection to Malachi Mede?

A creak behind her was the only warning that someone had snuck up behind her. Xandie shoved the ticket in her pocket and spun to face her intruder.

"Always poking your nose in where it isn't supposed to be." Chief of Police, Zach Braun, frowned at Xandie. "Do I even want to know why you're in here?"

Xandie made a point of poking under the desk in the corner of the room. "Looking for a runaway pug. If I don't find him, Elspeth will go on a hex rampage."

The chief looked over his shoulder, obviously scanning for a scary haggish witch. "Well, there's no pug here. How about you run along and keep out of my investigation?"

His investigation? *Ha. Let's see whose investigation it is.* Xandie smiled sweetly, took a leaf out of Hannah's blonde bombshell book, and sashayed out, wiggling her fingers in a sarcastic little wave. She could hear Zachy 'Bear' Braun grinding his teeth as she walked past.

Life was good when she could annoy a bear shifter and solve a murder at the same time.

SEVEN

"There's no need to be nervous. You know what to do," Winifred mumbled, looking anywhere but at Xandie.

"But I don't know. We were supposed to practice, but Elspeth whipped Colin away for some obscure reason. So, what do I do?" Okay, now she *was* nervous. Xandie paced alongside the show ring. The next stage was something called the gate stage.

"I was actually speaking to Colin." Winifred offered a weak smile to her niece. "We've gone through everything with him. Follow his lead."

"Yeah, this is a piece of cake, sugar. I got this. Follow me." Colin puffed out his manly doggy chest.

Xandie rolled her eyes. "This round is about Colin following my lead, my directions. Correct?"

Xandie waited for Colin to nod. "Then how can I follow him?"

Winifred and Colin looked at each other and then back to Xandie, speechless.

"Oh, for God's sake." Xandie raised her hands up in the air and let them drop heavily by her side.

Winifred grabbed Xandie's hands and gave them a quick squeeze. "Trust us. We have this managed." She rolled her eyes to the left side of the ring and then waited for Xandie's response. Frowning, Winifred rolled her eyes again to the left side.

Had her aunt suffered some kind of seizure no one had told her about? Then she followed her aunt's eye roll and scanned the left side of the ring. Mostly onlookers and supporters stood chatting ringside, waiting for the next stage to start. A few familiar faces from around town, but no one special...

Xandie's gaze stuttered to a stop and then reversed back two people. Hanging out ringside, with a gray wig and hunched over a walking stick, was her grandmother, Elspeth. Even banned, she'd come disguised as an old woman. *The irony.*

She blew out a breath and glared at her aunt. "Do I want to know what's going on?"

"Best not to. The future police report and all that." Colin winked at Xandie.

Davros popped up next to Colin. "All ready to go?"

"The engine is revving. Let me at those judges."

"Good to know. Wait for your cue, then slay the judges with your awesomeness." Davros winked at Colin and darted off to the next competitor.

"Shake your tail, sweet cheeks. Time to show the world my glorious, talented body." Colin trotted off and lined up at the edge of the ring.

"Elspeth owes me. Got it?" Xandie narrowed her gaze. "I will collect, and my fee will be double if it includes Elspeth danger time."

Winifred looked confused. "You aren't charging anything. You don't have a showing fee."

"Exactly." Xandie stomped off. Her threat hadn't exactly come out the way she wanted, but still, having a lurking Elspeth Harrow around didn't bode well.

Alex Pennywort, host extraordinaire, sidled up to Xandie as she stood behind Colin.

"Ms. Meyers?"

Xandie smiled up at the tall, skinny show host with his slicked-back hair and pale complexion and tried not to look too eager. Pennywort was on her interview list, and here he was in front of her. Maybe having Elspeth around wasn't bad luck. "Yes. But it's Xandie, please."

"I'm sorry to say, but there are some irregularities in Colin's paperwork."

Bam! There's the Harrow bad luck kicking in. "What kind of irregularities?"

Alex cleared his throat. "His birthdate was listed as last week, and his breed is noted down as 'whatever the hell I say it is.'"

Elspeth. "My grandmother's idea of a joke. Colin is a pug bonded to Elspeth Harrow and as such is blessed with some advantages." *And disadvantages.*

Pennywort glanced down at the pug currently sharpening his claws on a Stymphalian bird while chatting her up. The Greek bird had a beak of bronze and sharp, metallic feathers that gleamed in the sun. *And they're man-eaters.*

Xandie closed her eyes for a moment. Seriously, which pantheon of gods had she annoyed to get Colin-sitting duty?

The host stepped behind Xandie. "Flora is quite particular about her bronze feathers. She's been known to shoot them out like arrows at people who annoy her." Pennywort prudently moved a few more steps away from Colin and Xandie.

A bird with a beak and feathers made out of

bronze would interest Colin. Of course, any female with a heartbeat would do that.

"Colin, heel." Xandie snapped her fingers and prayed to her library that he'd listen.

Colin yanked his head around and scowled at Xandie but still moved away from the bird with a wink.

She offered a weak smile to the green-haired nymph standing behind Flora, the fierce metal bird. Xandie turned back to Pennywort and apologized to both the host and the nymph. "Sorry, Colin's just friendly. Everyone loves him. So, is it still okay for him to compete?"

Alex cleared his throat and checked his papers. "Of course. Now that you've explained, records will be amended. No problem." Alex paused for a moment, obviously measuring his words. "I heard you're investigating LaRue's death?"

Seriously? Gossip got around quicker than her grandmother did. "I'm not investigating, the police do that. I'm making sure my Aunt Amelia isn't charged with a crime she didn't commit."

"Of course." He nodded sagely and then lowered his voice. "After this stage is completed, come find me. I have information that might help you."

He winked slowly to make sure she got the point.

And then quick-stepped away to the middle of the ring. Clapping his hands and then flicking his fingers in a strange pattern, his voice boomed out as if he were speaking into a loudspeaker.

"Welcome one and all to the gate stage of the Supernatural Pet and Familiar Show. This is where our experienced judges will ask our competitors and their animals to complete a series of actions." He paused for dramatic effect, then plowed on. "Each competitor has an arm band with a number. The judges will call out a number and an action. The competitor will step forward with their animal and complete this action. At the end of the stage, if the judge calls out your number, you will step out and stack your dog to be judged. The winners will be announced shortly afterward. The judge today will be Wallace Moonshadow." With a flourish, Penny-wort welcomed the judge to the ring.

Xandie whispered down to Colin. "What does stack mean?"

"Pose me, baby. Show my muscles off and blind that wannabe accountant with my awesome show dog skills."

We're screwed.

The short, balding man with the nervous twitch stepped up to the ring. Moonshadow cleared his throat. "All competitors please move around the ring in a single pass until back in your starting spot." The animals shuffled around, but no one moved. Xandie craned her neck around the green nymph to see who was at the start.

A visibly sweating Lulu Moon crouched down next to the trembling Angora rabbit, currently glowing a fluorescent purple.

"Bunny has performance anxiety. Good chance for us to scoop the winning pool." Colin smirked and panted, obviously raring to go.

Green nymph agreed. "Moon's been off her game since LaRue stole her husband. Plus, being the second favorite to take out supernatural all breed champion is a tough weight to deal with."

Lulu stood, and taking this as her sign, the purple bunny took off like a rocket, previous anxiety apparently forgotten.

The line surged as competitors and their animals paraded around the ring.

"Showtime, baby. Try to keep up." Colin strutted, his short curly tail quivering in excitement with every step.

Xandie slipped to the right side, copying the nymph ahead of her. Colin was now closest to the judge. She had to admit the pug was behaving. In fact, he looked like he was having fun. Back arched, little tail bouncing. Even his ears were perky. Good old Colin was having the time of his life. As long as Elspeth stayed out of the way, their luck might hold.

Colin continued to parade around the ring and even winked at a few old women watchers, causing giggles to break out. Reaching his original spot again, Colin sat to attention at Xandie's feet.

Wallace conferred with Pennywort, then nodded. Stepping forward, the host's voice boomed out again. "Wow, what a field. Tough decision. But these numbers please step forward. One, six, nine, and finally, eleven."

"March, human. We're number eleven." Colin trotted out to stand at the end of a now very short line.

She followed, in shock. The pug had actually made the finals in the gate stage. Stopping behind Colin, Xandie wondered what came next.

The judge stepped up next to Pennywort. "Finalists, please spread out. Once settled, I will ask each animal at a time to strike a pose or stack." The judge went down the line, spending five minutes watching each animal pose and then noting something down on the paperwork before moving on.

Xandie whispered to Colin, carefully not moving her mouth too much. "What's your pose?"

"Magnificent, sweet cheeks. That's my pose."

The judge pulled up in front of Xandie, indicating that Colin should move into position.

Nodding to Colin, she held her breath.

Colin seamlessly flowed into an upright position. His legs straight and slightly apart, his head and ears back. Tail motionless. His eyes twinkled, his purple-spot-free fur gleaming golden brown.

Oh, yeah. He's got this.

Nodding, the judge stepped back, and Colin slid into line again.

Consulting with Pennywort, the judge handed him the paperwork and spoke to the competitors. "It's my pleasure as the judge for this year's SPAFS to announce the winner of the gate section of the show. The winner is Colin, owned by Elspeth Harrow, shown by Xandie Meyers. Step forward to receive your ribbon."

Xandie shared a shocked look with Colin and followed him to the judge, who slid a ribbon onto Colin's collar.

A screeched 'yes' from the crowd reached Xandie's ears. But she refused to look, as she knew Elspeth would be behind the scream.

Lulu Moon sagged as Xandie and Colin trotted past her and the bunny during their victory lap.

"One all, baby. That purple appetizer and I are level pegging in ranking now. Next stage is agility and then talent is final. But for now, it's red meat and fat cigars to celebrate."

Xandie led Colin into Winifred's sweaty hands. "No smoking for you, champ. Have to maintain your healthy coat."

"Spoilsport," Colin murmured as Winifred smothered him in kisses.

"I knew you could do it. Elspeth will be over the moon." Winifred kissed Colin again.

"Man, watch that tongue, Fred. I'm not into two-legged dames."

Winifred drew back, flustered. "I have to find Elspeth to let her know."

"I don't think that's a problem." Xandie pointed to the crowd of onlookers.

Elspeth, wig still intact, danced a jig, previous injuries from first stage judging and her old woman disguise completely forgotten.

Winifred dumped Colin on Xandie. "I have to calm her down before she has a witch attack or the shifter security ejects her. She's banned and isn't supposed to be on the grounds." Winifred sped off.

"Good luck with that." Xandie snickered and then hefted Colin up onto her hip. "How about we get you back to the grooming tent and give you a brush down?"

"Bring it on. My magnificence needs upkeep."

Rolling her eyes, Xandie entered the grooming tent. None of the other competitors had made it back yet. Dumping Colin on a table, Xandie grabbed a brush from Amity Puffin's treatment room.

The police tape had disappeared, and everything appeared normal except for the fact Amelia stood whispering to Lulu.

"Aunt Amelia? What are you doing here?"

Stiffening at her niece's voice, she passed something to Lulu before turning around. "Xandie, I hear congratulations are in order?"

"Thanks, but you didn't answer my question?"

Amelia faltered for a moment. "I had to come and make sure you're okay. That's all."

Elspeth was right, her daughter didn't take after her. Because that lie had been pitiful. "The real reason?"

Lulu stormed past Amelia and slapped a medicine packet back into the vet's hands. "She's a meddler. That's why. Can't leave the show alone."

"You push her too much, she'll collapse on you. Trust me. You'll regret it."

"All I regret is speaking to you again." Lulu slammed past Xandie and out of the treatment room.

"You need to stay out of this, Aunt Amelia. If the police got wind of this, you'd be back in jail for harassment."

Amelia dropped the medicine packet down on a nearby table and ran a hand over her shoulder-length, gray-streaked auburn hair. "I know, but I can't stand seeing animals being mistreated. She puts too much pressure on her Angora."

Xandie steered Amelia out of Lulu's way and into the cool sun of lunchtime in Maine. "Go home. I'll update you when I have something. Now get."

Nodding, Amelia left grudgingly, heading toward the food tent.

Sighing, Xandie stomped back inside.

"I swear if she doesn't back off, I'll report her to the cops." Lulu stood in front of Xandie, whatever Amelia had given her now clasped tightly in her fisted hand.

"Amelia means well, she wants the animals to be happy."

Grunting, Lulu stashed whatever she'd been holding into a box next to her caged Angora rabbit.

"She's nosy. My rabbit is fine. I just want her to leave me alone."

"Your rabbit did well out there," Xandie offered.

"Made it to the final until your dog stole the show." Lulu eyed a now snoring Colin. "Would you be willing to breed him?"

"To a rabbit?" Xandie tried not to look horrified, but it was a fight. These show people were freaky.

Lulu jerked back. "To another dog, you idiot. Seriously, how you got this far is beyond me."

Thank God for small mercies. "I'm not the owner. It's up to my grandmother. And the reason I got this far is because Lorelei isn't here competing, I guess." *Open up the interrogation bait...*

Sniffing, Lulu rearranged her grooming brushes. "LaRue not being here is a bonus for all of us."

"You didn't like her, did you?"

Lulu let loose a grating laugh. "No. She had an affair with my husband. He left me. Only to be dumped for that mouthy host, Alex Pennywort. Karma, I call it."

"You're happy to see her dead?"

She stopped and considered Xandie for a moment as other competitors filed into the tent. "I wouldn't say that, but I'm glad she's not competing.

And if you're thinking I'm the killer, don't. There's plenty of other people here with motive as well."

"Like whom, exactly?" *Keep on spilling details, Moon.*

"That judge, Velma Mystic, for one. They've known each other for a long time, and Velma knows something more, I'm sure of it. And Lorelei was attempting to leach onto the other judge, Noble Myrddin. Trust me, she was barking up the wrong tree there. But I didn't kill her." Lulu banged down a grooming brush. "I hated her, but I didn't want her dead. I wanted to slaughter her in the competition, not in real life."

Xandie backed away as Lulu's voice rose. "Okay then. Thanks for that information." Spinning around, she marched back to a waiting Winifred.

"What was all that about? She sounded angry."

"Missed opportunities for revenge, I think. But at least I have a few more suspects to add to my list."

Winifred nodded determinedly. "That's good work. We don't need to compete until tomorrow now. There are only novelty events for the rest of the day. We have some breathing space."

"You mean investigating space, don't you?" Xandie had a feel for the competition now and for the whackos, a.k.a. suspects, competing in it.

But the next step was tracking down the host, Alex Pennywort. He might have some juicy information. "Aunt Win? Any clue where the host went? I thought I'd ask him some questions."

"Probably in his tent? The judges had to share, but Mr. Pennywort has his own. It's on the other side of the judges' tent."

Xandie waved a hand in thanks and wandered off in the direction Winifred had described. As a host of the pet show, Pennywort had close contact with all the competitors and their fans. Maybe he'd noticed something that might help her narrow down a suspect. Xandie paused at the entrance to the tent. High-pitched humming emanated out. Did the show host have a giggling, girly competitor inside? She cleared her throat.

The tent flap opened, and Alex Pennywort stood there, gargling a mouthful of water.

"If you have company, I can come back another time?"

Swallowing, Alex motioned Xandie inside. "Just myself. I'm practicing vocal exercises. Helps loosen my vocal cords and make sure they don't get strained. Important in my line of work." He pointed to a seat next to his makeup table. "Please sit, Ms. Meyers."

The feminine humming had actually been

Pennywort himself? Not the picture of sartorial elegance the man normally presented. "You wanted to speak to me?"

Alex Pennywort cleared his throat and nodded. He paced in front of Xandie. "I normally try to stay out of the competitors' shenanigans. Relations can get quite strained, especially amongst the front runners."

He was talking about LaRue. "Lorelei and Lulu Moon, you mean?"

"They hated each other. Especially after LaRue stole Moon's husband and then threw him away. Poor Lulu was quite obsessed with grinding that woman into the ground."

She wasn't the only one. Lorelei had a multitude of enemies and victims. "Figuratively or literally?"

Alex looked flustered and ran a finger around the collar of his shirt. "I'm sure Lulu would never consciously hurt Ms. LaRue. She was just very angry."

Trying another tactic, Xandie smiled. "Of course, anyone would be. Did you notice anyone else who had a grudge against her?"

"Well... I'm not sure." He coughed and looked around the room wildly. When no distraction appeared, he collapsed into a chair next to Xandie and dropped his head into his hands with a moan.

Jackpot. Xandie fixed a stern expression on her face. "Mr. Pennywort, it would be better if you come clean with me before Police Chief Braun hunts you down."

"I'm weak," Pennywort wailed. "She played on my vanity."

"Another hair growth potion?" Like George Moon?

He shook his head. "I'm part troll." Alex peered anxiously into the mirror propped up on his makeup table. "My skin has a horrible swamp green tinge to it normally. I'm the host of all international SPAFS competitions. I have to look my best."

Blackmail again. Predictable. "Let me guess. She provided you with a potion for your skin. If you paid up."

He turned away from the mirror and shook his head. "I would have paid anything, but she didn't want cash. She wanted top billing."

"Top billing is..."

"She had to be the first in every stage. The leader of the competition like the star she was." Alex looked shamefaced. "Her words, not mine. I knew I shouldn't do it, but it seemed like such a little thing."

Blackmail was never little. "Did she put pressure on you to influence the judges?"

Pennywort lifted his chin. "I refused. She didn't like it but agreed to an introduction to one of the judges."

Xandie bet she knew exactly which judge. "Noble Myrddin?"

"Yes, him. I could have told her she had no chance, but she was so focused she wouldn't listen."

Xandie leaned over and patted the man on his boney shoulder. "Thanks for letting me know, Mr. Pennywort. I have one last question for you."

He braced himself.

"Did you kill Lorelei LaRue?"

"No way. Her potion worked wonders. I would never have jeopardized that. Thankfully, I have a few more potions left. An alchemist friend of mine has offered to reverse engineer it. I'll be fine."

Not worried about a dead blackmailer at all. Compassion, thy name was not Pennywort. "Thanks for answering my questions." Xandie stood and shook the host's hand.

"I feel much better now. Please keep the troll issue between us." He tapped the side of his nose and winked.

Internally shuddering, Xandie slipped out of his tent into the weak sunlight.

"Ms. Meyers?" he called after her.

If this was another skincare related confession, she was going to get Elspeth to hex his moisturizer.

"I wanted to wish you luck with the show." With a curt nod, he dropped the tent flap and disappeared back inside.

Why did she get the feeling she and Colin would need a truck full of karma goody points to survive the murderous competition?

EIGHT

"I want my money. She owed me. Now you owe me."

Xandie frowned as she heard the gruff words. She'd had a date for lunch with Aunt Winifred in the catering tent when her aunt realized she'd left her glasses behind in the grooming tent. Offering to grab them, Xandie had hotfooted it back and was now on the return journey. But the words she'd heard were more tantalizing than a sit-down lunch catered by Lila's mortal enemy.

"I told you. It's nothing to do with me. Lorelei was the gambler, not me. Her debt died with her."

Xandie's ears perked up at the sound of Amity Puffin's pleading voice.

"You and Lorelei were thick as thieves. Even went to the track with her. Pay the debt off or..."

"Or what?" Amity's voice wobbled.

"Or everyone finds out what you did for nasty Lorelei LaRue. Pay me my money or the truth comes out."

Xandie peered carefully around the back of the food tent to get a better look at Amity's debt collector. An older man with a dirty beard stood a full head shorter than Amity. That said, menace oozed out of his every pore.

Amity shrank back as the man flicked her shoulder and snickered to himself.

What a douche. Xandie purposefully shuffled her feet.

The man cursed and dropped out of sight around the corner.

Amity sagged against a tent brace before wiping her face and taking a deep breath. "Who's there?" she called out.

"Xandie Meyers." Xandie moved into view.

"Oh, Xandie. Hello. I wanted to say congratulations on Colin's win."

The words came out stilted, but the emotion on her face was real. Amity was genuinely congratulating her and Colin. "Thanks. It was all Colin. He's a born poser."

Amity forced a smile and nodded. "He likes being the center of attention."

"Are you okay? That guy looked nasty."

Amity brushed Xandie's concern away. "Oh. It's fine. He's a connection of Lorelei's."

"You mean her bookie?"

Amity reared back from Xandie. "No. Nothing like that. He's…"

"Her bookie and debt collector and now he wants the money from you."

"Yes." Breaking down, Amity grabbed Xandie's arm and sobbed. "He wants me to pay the debt off because Lorelei and I were friends. But I have no savings. The show only pays me a pittance for my services."

"Were you friends though? It sort of looked like she was ordering you around more than anything."

Letting go of Xandie's arm, Amity dropped onto a raised pile of decorative garden rocks beside a flag-stone path. "Lorelei isn't…" Amity corrected herself. "…wasn't a bad person. She was dirt poor as a kid and determined to never be in that spot again. But she was a gambler and loved the racing corns. She was up and down financially all the time."

"And Lorelei owed her bookie when she died?"

Amity nodded dejectedly. "A lot. Now he wants me to pay it."

"Why did you stay? She wasn't exactly the nicest person on the show circuit."

"Originally, she...uh." Amity stopped, and then in a rush of words blurted the rest out. "She blackmailed me into working as her assistant at first. She caught me doping some of my clients' animals so they'd have an edge against their competitors." Amity hung her head before staring Xandie in the face. "Lorelei was a force of nature. Sure, she took what she wanted, but she worked hard for it. No one but me knows just how hard. After a while, I happily worked for her. We were friends." Amity teared up again.

LaRue had blackmailed Amity to work for her. Who else was on Lorelei's hit list?

"How many other people did Lorelei blackmail?"

Amity winced. "A few. She had a diary she kept all her appointments and meetings in. And the dirt that she had on people. She made up a little code-name for people."

Bingo. That might have been the reason she died. Find that diary and find the killer. "Do you know where it is? The diary, I mean?"

"No clue. But she carried it everywhere she went. I know it wasn't among her possessions when the police went through them."

Xandie nibbled on the edge of her lip. She had to find that diary, but Winifred would want her glasses. Xandie needed to wrap this up, get back to her aunt, and go search for the diary. "Do you know the other blackmail victims?"

"George, I think. She had something he wanted and that judge, Myrddin. She had something juicy on him, but I don't know if she'd approached him yet. I do know there was someone she called her big score, but Lorelei never mentioned a name."

Xandie nodded, running potential suspects through her head. "Look, Amity, the best thing you can do if that nasty man comes looking for you is to tell Chief Braun. He'll help you. Lorelei's gone. Don't risk your life protecting a dead woman. Maybe leave the show for a while and keep a low profile. Take care." Xandie backtracked away from the dejected Amity. Talk about making the wrong life choices. Xandie shook her head. Lorelei was an unwanted gift that kept on giving even after death.

Xandie paused outside the food tent. A weird keening was coming from inside.

Colin pushed past Xandie but put the brakes on

when he spotted her. "You do not... I repeat. *Do. Not. Want* to go in there."

"Don't tell me you let loose with wind again?"

"No." Colin looked indignant for a moment. "Not this time, anyway. No, everyone's sick. Some nasty vegetable dish I didn't eat. Now they're all yakking non-stop. Hate to be on the cleaning team. I'm heading back to grooming and the sweet scent of my own belches." Colin bolted without a sideways glance.

Surely it can't be that bad? Xandie walked in. The stale odor of rancid meat and sweet, rotting milk slapped her in the face. She fought her own gag and placed a hand over her mouth, taking shallow breaths. *It's that bad.* The inside of the tent looked like a vomit-strewn battleground. Chef Luna ran around with a bunch of water bottles and towels, frantically shoving them at people.

"Help me. I have no clue what's going on. One minute they're eating, the next..." The chef swept a hand around the tent at the crowd of retching people.

Xandie bolted out of the tent and grabbed the closest body walking past. She recognized Malachi Mede only after she'd yanked him over to her. "I need you to get a hold of Chief Braun and organize doctors and healers here ASAP."

He paled. "What's going on now?"

"Looks like food poisoning."

He swore. "I knew it was a terrible idea to hire that Luna woman. She doesn't have the best reputation as a team player, but Hannah insisted because of the woman's drive for excellence. I'll get hold of Braun straight away." He took off at a run before coming to a halting stop and turning back. "Is Hannah inside? Is she okay?"

Xandie shrugged. "I've no clue, but I'll check. Grab Braun and the healers as quick as you can."

Mede nodded and took off running again.

Taking a deep breath, Xandie went in to find Winifred.

Gingerly stepping over rivers of vomit and heaving bodies, she searched for her aunt. Xandie heard her name whispered as she searched a darkened corner. Peering under a table, she squatted down. "Aunt Win? You okay?"

"Stay there. You shouldn't see your aunt like this." Winifred wailed and then followed with a violent rotting milk burp.

"I sent someone for Braun and the healers. Are you able to tell me what happened?"

"That annoying, loudmouth chef happened." Hannah Mede whispered from next to a slumped and moaning Winifred. "She served up this creamy vegetable dish. Ten minutes later, everyone's sick." Hannah hiccupped and wiped her mouth. "I only had a little, so I'm better off than some, unlike poor Winifred."

"It was so good and then *so* bad." Winifred leaned over, her plump frame looking deflated.

"Xandie," Hannah whispered even lower. "I saw Amelia outside the back of the food tent. Luna did too. I wanted to give you a heads up in case anyone accuses her." Hannah rubbed Winifred's back as she shook and heaved.

"Thanks, Hannah." Just what the Harrows needed. Next thing, there'd be an accusation of food sabotage from Luna.

"Get out of my way. I don't care if I'm banned. My daughter's in here." Elspeth, followed by Amelia, stormed past the chef, and tiptoed around the vomiting victims until they reached Xandie. "Here." Elspeth shoved a flask to Winifred and Hannah. "Drink up."

Hannah chugged a mouthful down right away while Winifred eyed the flask suspiciously.

"Mother. Not to be ungrateful, but what's in it?"

"You accuse your own mother of poisoning misdeeds?" Elspeth flung her gray-wigged head back in dramatic offence but relented when Winifred heaved again. "Fine, a little ginger, lemon, sugar, water and some goldenseal for the infection."

"And?" Winifred pressed her mother as the vial hovered near her lips.

"A little Witchshine for taste."

"Thank God." Winifred chugged the concoction back. A few minutes later, the spasms eased.

"Thanks, Elspeth." Xandie smiled gratefully at the elder Harrow. Witch healing brews were not her grandmother's forte. Spell books of death, maybe.

"Mede ran straight to Braun, and Aggie rang me. I had a general antidote on hand and came straight down."

"Why would you have an antidote on hand? What have you done, Elspeth?"

"Please, Xandie. The key word is *general*. It doesn't hurt to have a general, long-lasting antidote. In case." Elspeth waggled a hand around the room. "If I'd poisoned this lot, the police would cart out body bags, not dodge projectile vomiting."

A white-coated healer leaned down next to Elspeth. "Can I help anyone? We have antidotes available."

"Whack off, nosy. No one doses my daughter and her friends but me. Besides, who do you think supplied the antidote?" Elspeth snarled at the young healer.

"It's okay, Sophie. I've got it from here." Aggie Braun, matriarch of the Braun shifter clan and police dispatcher, patted the healer on the shoulder and then shooed the young woman away. "Ignore her. She got her healer license last month. She's so excited to see people vomiting, every sane thought went out of her ears." Aggie leaned down and hoisted Hannah up. "Upsy daisy, Hannah girl. Let's get you out of this diseased hole. No offense."

Hannah wobbled. "None taken. I'm thinking I made an enormous mistake coming back to Point Muse, anyway."

Aggie guided Hannah into the waiting arms of her husband. "You aren't the first person who's said that about this town."

"Hannah," Malachi Mede cried out and clutched his wife close. "Are you okay?"

Hannah shoved herself away and scowled at her husband. "I emptied the contents of my stomach. *In public.* How good could I be?" Hannah stomped out of the vomit-filled tent toward the resort in her bare feet, stilettos forgotten. Malachi stumbled after her.

Xandie turned back to her aunts and grandmother. "I don't think you'll be seeing the Medes here again in a hurry."

"Well, they do say you can never go back." Winifred wobbled as she stood.

"This town is cursed. Did you hear me? I told the organizers when they confirmed Point Muse as a locality that we would regret it. I was right." The female judge, Velma Mystic, still holding a bucket in one hand, patted an askew red wig with the other.

"Shut up, Mystic. You're a fake. We all know it," Elspeth growled at the woman.

Velma climbed on a chair and yelled over the top of the vomit victims and healers still administering the antidote, "Point Muse is a cursed town. Things always go wrong here. And now a killer walks amongst us. I've seen the blood and death in a vision."

The judge, Moonshadow, lifted his head from the table he'd face planted on. "Can't someone shut up that loud woman? Haven't we suffered enough?"

Ignoring her fellow judges' heckling, Mystic put a hand over her handbag and caressed it for a moment. "Lorelei was a close friend, and I've spoken to the poor departed Fifi. Even in death, she protects her mistress, but I now know who killed her and why." Velma wavered on the chair before crashing off the side and onto the ground.

Healers rushed to the distraught woman, and three burly men were called in to carry her out, seemingly senseless. Although Xandie was sure if Velma was knocked out, her eyes wouldn't be open a crack, and she'd have released the stranglehold on her handbag.

"What a ham. Charlatans like her give us witches a bad name." Elspeth spat on the floor. "Now, I wonder how many competitors will pull out?"

"Compassion, Gran, compassion." Xandie ignored her grandmother's antics and helped Winifred outside into the fresh air.

Lila rushed up with a tired Amelia in tow. "I heard on the police scanner about the vomit comet. Thought I'd see if you guys are okay?"

"Thanks to Elspeth, we are. I missed the food poisoning, but Aunt Win caught it head on." That reminded Xandie. She grabbed Winifred's glasses from her pocket and handed them over. "I got delayed by Amity Puffin and Lorelei's bookie, that's why I didn't eat."

"Lucky," Winifred murmured. "But at least Colin didn't eat either." Winifred looked around, then squeaked in dismay when the normally ravenous pug failed to appear.

"Don't stress. He bolted for the grooming tent when the vomiting started. He's probably snoring by now," Xandie offered.

Elspeth stowed her empty vials of antidote away in voluminous pockets, then clapped her hands. "I doubt whether the competition will resume today. I'll take him home for a bubble bath. He loves getting in with me. Tata, girlies." Elspeth sauntered away.

As one, Lila and Xandie shuddered. Not a picture one wanted in one's head.

"You. How dare you show your face here after what you did." Chef Madelyn pointed a quivering finger at the Harrow women.

Xandie stepped in front of Lila. "Lila had nothing to do with this."

"I know she didn't, but her mother did. I had to duck out of the food tent for a moment, and when I came back, she was lurking around."

Amelia shook her head. "Why would I hurt anyone or make my own sister sick?"

"Because you're a Harrow. You probably have some devious plan in play. You might even get back at me for your own daughter ruining my good name."

"From what I've heard, you already have a reputation for not being a team player." Xandie glowered at the chef. No way was anyone accusing her family. Besides, if it were anyone, it would have been Elspeth. Aunt Amelia didn't have it in her.

"Lies. Harrow lies." Luna hissed her words, spit flying with a spray of vitriol. "You mark my words. We'll see another body yet." The woman stomped off, outrage causing her chef's hat to quiver.

Xandie shivered. Somehow the crazy cook's words had a ring of foreshadowing to them.

She needed to find the killer, before Chef Luna was proven right. If she didn't, they'd find another body.

This pet circuit was a killer.

NINE

Elspeth hadn't been joking about the bath. Lila had sent horrible, horrible photos. Her cousin called it proof of psychosis and was stockpiling evidence for a future committal to Eternal Springs, Point Muse's equivalent of a supernatural retirement home. Xandie couldn't help but shudder. The image of Elspeth and Colin bathing together was just plain unnatural.

Xandie wandered toward the grooming tent, taking her time and mulling over events. Amelia still seemed too exhausted. She'd received an emergency call-out last night and arrived back home in the early hours, almost asleep on her feet. Thankfully, her aunt's receptionist had worked late as well and dropped Amelia home. At least her other aunt,

Winifred, was feeling perky. She'd rung Xandie at sunrise to go over their plan of attack for today's agility competition. Xandie was positive Colin would lose by a mile. His chubby pug body wasn't her image of agile.

"Leave me alone, damn you." Hannah Mede's faint tones carried on the wind. "Back off," she screeched.

That was much louder. Xandie bolted toward the bushland at the back of the resort where Hannah's voice had drifted from.

Point Muse was known for its beautiful coastline and natural scenery. Hiking tracks dotted the forested area that ringed one side of the town entrance, acting like a natural barrier. On the other side was a deep cold lake. The land Point Muse Springs Resort rested on tapered away into thick-forested conservation land.

Xandie ran full tilt toward Hannah, who was backed up against a tree trunk, jabbing at an animal with a stick.

"Hannah, are you okay?"

"I. Am. Not." Hannah turned her head and glared at Xandie. Her blonde ringlets stuck straight out, tangled with sticks, and a smear of dirt coated one cheek. The animal lunged, snapping at Hannah's feet. Squealing, she jabbed the stick out again.

Fox. That's what the animal was. Some kind of fox, a flame-red one with a narrow face, white-tipped tail, and piercing yellow eyes. Xandie crouched and grabbed a small rock. Those bright gold eyes carried a smidge too much knowledge and awareness. In a town of supernatural witches, demons, pixies, and shifters, what were the odds she was looking at a fox shifter? "Hannah, get ready to run over here."

Hannah telegraphed are-you-crazy through her eyes to Xandie. "Okay."

Xandie hefted the rock and pegged it straight at the fox. It hit square on the animal's cheek. Letting out a shaky yelp, the shifter backed away.

Hannah limped toward Xandie, who stood prepared with another stone. The fox kept backing away, a small gash on its cheek bleeding somewhat. With one last yip at the women, the animal sped off into the trees.

Hannah slumped against Xandie. "Well, that's a half hour of my life I won't get back. Not to mention my blood the damn thing spilled." Hannah grabbed her pants leg and showed Xandie a small, bloody animal bite.

"Okay, that's yuck. Let's get you up to the resort. There'll be a first aid kit up there somewhere."

Hannah agreed and stumbled toward the resort until Xandie grabbed an arm and hoisted her weight a little. Making their way back at a snail's pace, Xandie quizzed Hannah. "What happened? Was that a fox? Maybe a vampire fox hungering for your blood?" Xandie paused for a breath.

"Whoa, conspiracy girl. Breathe. I have no clue where it came from. I went for a walk, and the next thing I know, a wild animal is stalking me, trying to take a mouthful outta me."

Xandie helped Hannah into the back of the resort kitchen. "Kinda weird that it didn't do more damage. It's almost like it was only trying to scare you."

Hannah pointed to a small hallway at the opposite end to Lorelei's dressing room. "That's my office. There should be a first aid kit or do we call Elspeth?"

"The less my grandmother is near the show, or open wounds, the better."

Hannah placed a hand on the doorknob, and then took it off, frowning.

"What's wrong?"

"I locked my office last night after the vomiting episode."

"Okay?"

"No, you don't get it. I locked up last night, but it's open now. See?" Hannah turned the doorknob and eased the door open a crack.

Xandie dropped Hannah's arm and moved in front of her. "Let me go first. You're already wounded." Xandie forced a smile. "Just in case."

Slipping inside the room, Xandie peered around. Someone had trashed the room. Shelves were tipped over and paperwork was strewn everywhere. The heavy wood desk was still in place. Xandie moved to right a tipped chair next to the desk and froze with a tiny squeak.

"You okay?" Hannah limped in, aghast at the state of the office. "See? I told you this resort is cursed. Now someone's broken in."

"It's worse than that." Xandie kneeled.

"What can be worse than a disorganized, trashed office?"

"A dead body."

"What?" Hannah squealed, but still peered over the desk. "Holy... That's Velma Mystic, one of the judges."

"Was, you mean." Xandie took her pulse, but the woman was definitely dead. Especially with one side of her head covered in blood and a cracked crystal ball lying next to her.

"Xandie? Didn't Velma proclaim yesterday she knew who the killer was?"

"She did. And it looks like she was right. Someone didn't want her to talk." Xandie searched around and found Velma's handbag tucked under the desk. She searched inside for Lorelei's diary. She bet that was why Velma wouldn't let her handbag out of her sight in the catering tent yesterday. Xandie didn't believe Velma's assertions that the dearly departed Fifi had told her about the killer. More likely Velma had found LaRue's diary.

"That's Lorelei's." Hannah pointed to a gauzy purple scarf sitting in the bottom of Velma's purse. "See, it's got the purple and pink sparkle polish staining it. I remember that horrible woman yelling at Amity when she painted Fifi's nails."

Velma had likely found the dead woman's diary, so where was it now? "We need to let the police chief know what happened."

Hannah nodded. "I'll send one of the reception staff for the chief. I can trust him to keep his mouth shut." Hannah limped out, leaving Xandie alone with the body.

Velma must have discovered the killer, and that

person had killed her for it. The only silver lining, depending on the time of death, was that Amelia had been working on a sick patient last night. Poor Velma might be her aunt's get-out-of-jail-free card.

"Why do I always find you leaning over a dead body?" Zach Braun grumped as he prowled into the room.

Xandie straightened. "It's a gift. And technically, it's inclining, not leaning. Velma Mystic's body proves my aunt wasn't involved."

The police chief crossed his arms and scowled at Xandie. "How does this poor woman's death prove anything? There's a killer in Point Muse, and a second body confirms the first death was definitely murder and not an accident."

Xandie gritted her teeth. Could this man annoy her anymore? "Amelia had an emergency call last night and was occupied for hours. She has witnesses. My aunt couldn't have been the killer."

"This time. Amelia might have an accomplice."

Snorting, she shook her head. "Since when do Harrows play well with others? This proves Amelia's innocence."

"That's not for you to decide. We'll interview any witnesses and examine the body before determining if this clears your aunt."

"You know Amelia. She's not capable of this."

"Of course he does. But he just needs to follow protocol." Aggie strode in and handed Zach a large coffee from Lila's bakery, Heart's Delight. "Xandie is right about one thing. Your cousin, Sasha, was also called into the surgery last night around nine. She stayed with Amelia until around two am, when she dropped her back at Harrow House. I took a statement a little while ago."

Chief Braun slouched a little and dropped his arms. "Fine, but we still need to interview your aunt, Xandie. If you see her, please ask her to come in for a talk." Zach scowled. "Now, please leave my crime scene alone and deal with that evil pug of Elspeth's."

As much leeway from Zachy 'Bear' Braun as she was likely to get. Xandie straightened and wiped a hand on her jeans. She needed to find Colin anyway. Who knew what Elspeth and Winifred had planned for today? And she needed to make sure Hannah was okay after her weird fox attack. The library might even have some information for her. Plus, she needed to find that missing diary. "Well, I guess I'll leave this murder in your capable hands. Aggie." Ignoring

Zach, Xandie air kissed Aggie goodbye. As she moved away, Zach grumped to his mother about how no one respected his title.

Xandie snickered. When one had a mother as capable and hard-working as Agatha Braun, it must be hard to measure up.

The first person she ran into was her cousin, Lila.

"Xandie, thank God. We heard you found another body." Lila grabbed Xandie and spun her around in a tight hug. "See, I told you all we needed was another body to prove Mom's innocence."

"Only if the evidence works in Aunt Amelia's favor. Aggie's on the Harrows' side, and that's half the battle." Xandie glanced around, but chaos and mayhem were currently on the down low. No Colin or Elspeth hanging around could be bad or good.

"Calm, Meyers. The agility stage is still on, but later in the afternoon. Between the vomiting yesterday and the murder today, they want to get the show done before anyone else dies. Agility today and last stage, talent, tomorrow. Then the announcement of the overall winner not long after. Colin and the purple angora rabbit are equal so far." Lila slapped Xandie on the back. "Almost done and then you can wash your hands of Colin, preferably with disinfectant."

Xandie grimaced but followed Lila out to the parking lot. "Only if I win. If I lose, I'll be hearing about it for a very long time."

"Only until Elspeth dies."

"She hexes people and snorts evil energy like a drug. How long do you think she'll last for?"

Lila unlocked the bakery van. "Excellent point. You'd better win."

Win the contest with a witch-tampered pug and find out who was killing contestants before her aunt ended up in jail or Xandie and Colin became the next casualties.

Piece of cake...

TEN

"Another body to add to your list. What a surprise." Theo rolled his eyes as he batted Horatio, his pet imp, around the floor.

"Not my fault. I'm not the killer." Xandie had scarfed some food and was now cleaning and shelving in the library before she headed back to the competition.

"You're a body magnet. Anyone would think *you* were the banshee obsessed with death, not your cousin."

"Holly isn't obsessed, it's her job." Xandie shelved two possessed scrolls that had chased the imp around the room earlier.

"You say tomato…" Theo snickered and dropped

Horatio before stretching out flat on the floor, legs waving in the air. "You could show some love."

Xandie wrinkled her nose. "*One,* you're not touchy-feely and prefer to be worshipped from afar. *Two,* I know you used to be an ancient Greek teenager. That's kind of off-putting."

"Fine." Theo sat upright. "But you better not leave me for that barking, four-legged monstrosity."

"Ha." Xandie snapped her fingers. "I knew it was pug jealousy."

Theo tilted his nose up in the air. "There's no such thing as pug jealousy. But if there was, it would be reasonable, since you're spending all your time with him."

Finally, some librarian love from her snarky talking feline. Xandie crouched down and rubbed behind Theo's ears, dodging the paw he jabbed at her defenseless forehead. "Not leaving you, feline. Just undercover. I swear, Colin's hygiene habits have nothing on yours."

"Well, for the library's well-being, I think that's a smart idea."

Xandie straightened. *Speaking of the library.* "Library, what do you know of fox shifters?"

A fiery red book with black lettering flew across the room to drop with a bang at Xandie's feet.

"Thanks, library." Xandie blew it a kiss and flicked through the book. "Family lines and hierarchy of Kitsune migration," Xandie read aloud.

"In answer to your silent question, Kitsune are Japanese fox shifters. Each clan has different characteristics and coloring."

"Did you eat a dictionary on fantastical creatures? Or have you been lurking on Witchpedia?"

"I keep telling you, just because any old witch can change or add to the information doesn't make it any less reliable."

"Your addiction to the Witchweb discombobulates me."

"Now who swallowed a dictionary?" Theo sneered at Xandie.

Xandie ignored her petulant cat and ran through the contents page detailing the different clans. One name snagged her attention. *Shan.* Wasn't that the name of the businessman Malachi Mede had been having a secretive meeting with?

Xandie flipped to the Shan clan chapter and read out loud.

"The Shan Kitsune clan has origins dating back to the twelfth century when the clan settled in the mountainous regions of northern Japan. Kitsune are intelligent beings, with different clans possessing

unique abilities. All Kitsune possess the ability to shift between human and fox form. The Shan clan's Kitsune form is that of a red fox, with a white-tipped tail and yellow eyes and a narrow face. They do not resemble nine-tailed Kitsune as depicted within Japanese and Chinese mythology. The Shan clan's gifts are intelligence, long lives, and financial acumen, and they are gifted with finances and making money. The Shan are known for their shrewd wisdom in the property market. They own the Shan Resort Group, which is a resort chain catering to only supernatural customers. They are amongst the top five wealthy Kitsune clans."

Xandie pondered the fox shifter. *Why would Mr. Shan attack Hannah?* Shan was in the resort business. Was he here to convince the Medes to sell Point Muse Resort Springs?

"I know your furry book must be riveting, but you've got a body on the doorstep."

"What?" Xandie jumped up and raced to the front door, peering out.

"This one's alive and kicking at the moment, but I thought the word *body* added drama and impact. Plus, your wobbly butt got moving twice as quick." Theo snickered and galloped upstairs with Horatio hanging off the leather saddle on Theo's back like a cowboy.

Some days she could throttle her talking cat, but who knew who the library would saddle her with next? Xandie peered through her front window at the immaculately dressed Mr. Shan, resort owner and fox shifter. Her number one suspect.

"You aren't stepping inside my house, mister," Xandie muttered before grabbing her bag and stepping out, locking the front door behind her. Elspeth had given her an immobilizer hex ages ago. If Shan got out of hand, she'd hit him with it and run for help. Xandie acted surprised to see the shifter on her doorstep. "Why, Mr. Shan. What a surprise? Can I help you?"

The Japanese Kitsune bowed a greeting. "Not much of a surprise, considering you're probably already executing library research on my family name."

Xandie spotted a small slice on his cheek. "I notice you have a cut on your face. Hope nothing serious happened?" Xandie grinned with all of her teeth on show. *First salvo to her.*

Shan dropped his head back and guffawed, his polite officious image shattered. Recovering, he nodded. "Nothing serious, but kudos on your aim,

Ms. Meyers. I was impressed and I'm sure your actions relieved Mrs. Mede."

"Why bother to menace and intimidate her?"

"The Medes, or at least Malachi, is a friend of mine. I was helping him."

"You're beating around the bush. Cough it up. Why did you hurt Hannah?"

Shan looked affronted at Xandie. "I had no intention of hurting anyone. Sometimes the hunt can get out of hand. And Mrs. Mede was exerting too much prey response for a predator not to have a nibble."

"I'm sure Mede doesn't want you chewing on his wife."

"No. That wasn't the plan." Shan flicked an imaginary lint speck off his jacket. "Mrs. Mede has expensive taste, and sometimes people can get themselves into trouble when owing a debt to unsavory characters. I was shadowing her for her protection. But the incident got out of hand. I wanted to let you know so you could reassure Mrs. Mede that I meant no harm." He smiled a blinding white teeth grin.

And there was the charm offensive. Did he think she was stupid enough to fall for it? Or his lame explanation?

He produced a business card with a number on it. "If you need to ask me any more questions. *Any* questions. Please ring." Nodding, he wandered off toward an expensive silver car. He waved as he slipped into the car.

Wow, he thinks I'm susceptible to his charms. Xandie pocketed the card and pondered her next move. Colin's agility stage was next on the pet show agenda, but after that, she needed to speak to Hannah about her finances.

A detective's job is never ending.

Xandie wiped her sweaty palms against her jeans. Nerves were getting to her. She couldn't see Elspeth in disguise or out in the crowd anywhere. But the back of her neck burned, so she knew her grandmother was there somewhere, watching. At least she hoped it was Elspeth. ASP agents were still hanging around, but she hadn't spotted the black SUV again.

The judges, including the newly press-ganged Dorothy Johnson, octogenarian witch hairdresser, lined up at the agility ring, whispering.

The host, Alex Pennywort, conferred with the three judges, then stepped up. He performed his weird finger exercises again, and his voice boomed over the crowd. "Welcome to the agility section of our competition. This is the second to last stage, and we have had the recent addition of judge Dorothy Johnson to replace the late Velma Mystic, may she rest in peace." Alex bowed his head for a split second in a sort of respectful way but then clapped his hands to get started. "The judges in this round scrutinize the animal competitors on their ability to navigate various obstacles, both magical and non-magical, *without* handler interference."

The course looked easy enough. A tunnel, a dog walk, a jump, a teeter-totter, and a tire jump. The magical obstacles included a ring that hovered in the air for those that could fly. For those animals restricted to ground level, a small cloud of pixie dust, sparkling glitter particles, had been employed. The other side had weave poles, a pose table, and a collapsed tunnel. Magic wise, a wind jump hovered ten inches above the ground and bobbed up and down.

A puddle of fluorescent yellow magic sand was the final magical obstacle. The more magic the animal used, the quicker they sank.

Winifred had explained the rules—each refusal or dropped bar resulted in a time fault, totaled at the end of the course. Judges awarded points, taking into account all faults. Fewer faults meant more points and would equal a winning place.

Other competitors had placed small ornate canopies or awnings over the side of the agility ring for shade. A lot of them had sponsors' names emblazoned in glitter across the top.

"You sure you've got this?" Xandie asked Colin. *Again.* "The course looks complicated."

"Please. I could run this course blindfolded," he panted, raring to go.

Alex Pennywort cleared his throat. "Let's get to it. First competitor up to the starting area, please." Alex swept his hand over a taped-off area.

The purple angora bunny limped to the starting point. Lulu kneeled and patted the rabbit on her fluffy head before backing away. A low tone beep indicated the start. The bunny bounced off at a ferocious pace. Whatever anxiety the bunny had been experiencing over the last few days had evaporated. Xandie couldn't believe the change; maybe the bunny had turbo thrusters under that cute purple tail?

The rabbit made it through the first four mundane obstacles with no sweat but paused for a few seconds before charging into the purple pixie dust. The little animal thumped at it with big back paws until the dust disappeared and then hopped around to the other side of the ring, barely pausing at the non-magical obstacles until it reached the winged jump. Taking a bunny run-up, Princess threw herself at the jump. The jump fluttered out of the rabbit's reach and the animal hit the ground with a slam.

"I told you so. The bunny's cooked," Colin crowed to Xandie.

"Don't count your angora yet. Check it out." Xandie pointed to the rabbit.

The bunny adjusted her stride and took the jump again, nailing it this time. Without slowing down, Princess reached the final magical obstacle, the yellow sand. She launched herself into the air and cleared the sand with inches to spare. Lulu and the purple angora received a standing ovation.

Colin sniffed. "Wait until they see a real performer."

"Well, settle back. We're the last to compete. Four more animals ahead of us."

The host spoke to the judges for a moment as he consulted his papers. "Apologies, competitors and onlookers, but we have a stack of last-minute scratchings. There will now only be two competitors in total for the agility section."

"Better odds anyway."

Colin, always the optimist. "Right, that means you're on now. You got this, pug. Good luck."

"No need for luck, toots." Colin sauntered up to the start, then yawned, bone cracking wide. At the start tone, the pug confidently trotted out onto the course. He ambled through the tunnel but amped up his speed as he came through the other side, his little brown legs pedaling fast. Onto the dog walk and Colin balanced like a gymnast as he crossed. But as he approached the teeter-totter, his confidence wavered. He crept on but froze as the obstacle shifted forward and back.

"Come on, Colin. Come on," Winifred squealed from behind the edge of the ring.

Colin jerked as he heard her and swayed precariously on the obstacle, back legs scrabbling for balance. The crowd gasped as Colin forced one leg in front of the other until he cleared the other side.

Xandie crossed her fingers for luck. Colin had incurred a time penalty for wavering at the teeter-totter. He needed to nail the other obstacles to be in the running for first place.

Colin sped up, sailing through the tire jump. Ignoring the magical jump, he powered into the cloud of purple pixie dust. *Where he stayed.* The only part of Colin now visible was his drooping brown tail.

She covered her eyes. After Colin's reaction to Elspeth's potion that included pixie dust, she dreaded to think what the poor pug would look like on the other side of the dust cloud.

First one paw, then another appeared. Colin dragged himself out of the cloud, covered in nasty, glittering, purple patches. The pug picked up his pace and moved through the rest of the course until he hit the magical sand.

Xandie crossed her fingers behind her back as the crowd fell silent.

Colin backed away from the sand, carving a run-up. He took a deep breath and galloped as much as his gravity-heavy body would allow, then leaped. The pug sailed over the sand, his legs pedaling like he was riding a bike in the air.

He was going to make it. Xandie couldn't believe the pug got air. At least for a little while.

Then he dropped like a rock at the edge of the sand, paws scrabbling for solid ground. He slid back into the sand and let out a defeated groan as he disappeared.

Xandie slapped a hand over her mouth and darted toward the judges, ready to demand a rescue, but with a belching pop, the pug dragged himself out of the sand and collapsed on the ground, panting.

"Come on, Colin. Bring it home for the Harrows." Elspeth's pathetically disguised voice boomed over the spectators. With a shake, he pushed himself up, trotted across the finish line, and collapsed again.

Xandie bolted for her grandmother's mouthy pet. No matter how annoying the dog was, that course had exhausted the poor thing. Xandie crouched next to the pug. "You okay?"

He cracked open an eye and then let it fall closed. "Nailed it."

Xandie picked Colin up and then held him away from her body. "Phew. That sand stinks when mixed with pixie dust and eau de pug."

Winifred rushed up. "Brave Colin. A warrior's heart." She snatched the pug off Xandie and cuddled him to her chest regardless of the mess.

Colin let out a deep sigh and sagged against Winifred. "Bacon?" He let out a weak, pitiful groan.

"Whatever you need, Colin the magnificent."

Xandie rolled her eyes. The pug was working her aunt big-time.

Alex Pennywort conferred with the judges, then stepped forward. "The judges have conferred, and we have a clear winner. The judges award first place to Lulu Moon and her sparkle angora rabbit for winning the agility phase. Congratulations and commiserations for those who haven't placed. Now, the talent section is scheduled for tomorrow morning, with final judging in the afternoon." Pennywort bowed to the crowd before shuffling back to the judges.

"No." Elspeth jumped the ring, flinging her gray wig to the ground. "They robbed us, our win stolen. Didn't you see his masterful performance on the field?" Elspeth's eyes glowed amber.

Wolf shifters closed in on Elspeth. Hulking men in tight black security shirts would normally have Elspeth pinching up a storm, but at the moment, the stolen victory consumed the Harrow grandmother.

Elspeth spun around, hands outstretched. "You'll never take me alive, suckers." She smashed a small balloon on the ground. Red smoke wreathed her in small circles and grew thicker and thicker until it completely obscured her corner of the competing ring.

The shifters threw themselves at the smoke and disappeared from view. Until a wolf body flew out and landed smack bang in the magic sand. Three other wolves bounded out of the smoky haze, yelping and swiping at their furry noses.

Winifred, holding the pug, backed away. "Since I've got Colin, I'm afraid you're on crazy Harrow duty."

"She might've created me, but that dame's two mini corns short of a herd."

Xandie ambled toward the red cloud hiding her grandmother, but the spry old girl disappeared by the time she got there. Xandie took a lap around the tents to spot her delinquent family member but instead, ran across Davros and the judge, Wallace Moonshadow, arguing. Well, the judge was. Davros just rolled his eyes and tapped his clipboard.

"No more, Davros. First was that piece of work LaRue getting stoned. Then that traumatic vomiting event. I lost pounds, *pounds*. And now that weird old woman disappearing in a cloud of red smoke." Wallace crossed his arms. "SPAFS is not paying me for this level of drama. In fact, they aren't paying me enough at all."

"Now, now, Wallace, take a breath and remember we have a contract." Davros patted the man's shoulder.

"I'm positive murder breaks the contract." Moonshadow shook off the producer's hand. "I'll be in the judges' tent packing."

Davros waited for Moonshadow to leave and then pitched his clipboard at the side of the grooming tent, ducking as it rebounded back. "*Prima donna! Money hungry, egotistical, talentless hack,*" he squeaked.

Xandie picked up the abused clipboard. "Here."

Squealing in fright, the large man spun around and placed a trembling hand on his chest. "You have a talent for sneaking, Ms. Meyers."

Xandie handed the producer his precious clipboard. "Sorry, it's my devious Harrow genes."

Davros shuddered. "My nana was a poker crony of Elspeth's before she passed on. If you're half as effective as she is at scaring people, you'll be set in the sleuthing business."

"What about the blackmail one?" Xandie arched an eyebrow.

"*My, my.* We are direct, aren't we, sweetie?" Davros smirked at Xandie for a moment before sobering. "Yes, LaRue loved her blackmail. And no, she didn't tap me. I'm an open book, can't keep a secret to save myself. She would have struggled to find anything to pin me down on that wasn't common knowledge. But I was aware of her predilections, and as long as the show went on, I didn't care."

"And now?"

"Now we have a killer on the loose, competitors are dropping out like flies for fear they'll be next, and nothing is running on schedule. This place is a nightmare." He tugged at his curly brown hair with one hand and shook his clipboard with the other.

"Not happy in Point Muse?" Murder and mayhem *was* an acquired taste for most people, even supernatural ones.

He sniffed. "It's not Point Muse. My father grew up here. I don't have an issue with the town itself. It's this place and those Medes driving me crazy."

"You've had problems with the resort?" Davros was definitely an open book. Information poured out of him.

"Power outages, missing props, people falling, employees and competitors quitting without warning. Plus, those Medes are trying to micromanage everything. If I didn't know any better, I'd swear they were trying to make us pack up and leave."

"And would you?"

"I'd be out of here in a flash if it were up to me. But I'm a producer of this circus. The SPAFS

Corporation are notorious penny pinchers. They never cancel."

"Thanks, Davros. I appreciate your honesty."

"Eh." He shrugged. "Nana owed Elspeth a poker marker before she died. Consider this the family's repayment. Ciao." He waggled his fingers and left, yelling out for his minions as he went.

Xandie tapped her chin, deep in thought. That talk with Davros had been very interesting. Why would the Medes want to force SPAFS to cancel the pet show?

What would they get out of it?

ELEVEN

The red underneath her fingernails itched. Xandie scraped at the residue left over from her grandmother's smoke distraction.

"Good luck. Last time I put my hand in one of Elspeth's spells, the skin was zombie green for two weeks." Lila pegged a piece of the crust from her blueberry pie at Xandie.

Xandie snatched it out of the air and chomped it. "I don't get how an old woman is so fast on her feet. The shifters should have had her. Instead, she disappears."

"I'd say clean living, but this is Elspeth. Harvesting the death energy of her enemies? Who knows, but at least she's at home under lock and key for now."

Xandie glanced around Lila's quiet bakery. The late afternoon rush meant you had to line up if you wanted Lila's baked delights.

Lila followed Xandie's glance. "Been like this since the vomiting episode at the catering tent." She shrugged. "As soon as Luna and that damn show leave, all will be back to normal."

"*That show* will be the death of me. Between searching for a killer and dealing with Colin and Elspeth, I'm exhausted." Xandie slumped her head down on the table.

"One more stage to go. But with Colin down two to one, the best it will be is a draw. Mom told me it will go to a last stacking pose for a final decision."

Xandie raised her head. "Your mom talked about the show?"

"I know, scared me too. But she seems okay, other than being worried about who's marked for death next."

"I'm more concerned about keeping her out of jail and working out what Lorelei LaRue did to get herself murdered."

"I may be able to help with some of that." A dapper gentleman in an evening coat with a burgundy cravat stared down at Xandie.

Lila cleared her throat. "I'll leave you to it, cuz."

Xandie looked at the very well-dressed man. Skinny and tall with a shock of white-blonde hair, something familiar about him niggled at her. She snapped her fingers. "You're a judge for the show."

He bowed. "Myrddin. Noble Myrddin, at your service, Librarian Meyers," he said, his plummy English tones filling the air.

"Xandie is fine. How can I help you?" She waved at Lila's vacated chair. "You're welcome to sit."

"Thank you." He settled himself in the chair and then twitched his coattails back into place. "Since you're investigating the SPAFS murders, I did you the courtesy of approaching you first for my interview."

Courtesy? The English gentleman image clashed with Point Muse's air of teetering-on-the-edge-of-chaos atmosphere. "Why would I interview you, Mr. Myrddin?"

"Because that detestable LaRue tried to blackmail me." He made a face like he'd sucked a lemon.

What could this prim and proper man have done that was worth blackmailing? *It's always the quiet ones.* Xandie made an encouraging murmur.

"LaRue approached me the day before the show started. All bright-eyed and happy the entire time she was trying to blackmail me." He sniffed, disgust written across his face.

"If you don't mind me asking, what was she blackmailing you about?"

"*Trying*. Trying to blackmail me. One must be precise when dealing with this type of subterfuge. In my experience." Myrddin's smile twitched into something a little more devious.

"Okay, she was trying to blackmail you. Care to share why?"

Myrddin leaned on the table and smiled thinly at Xandie. "She found out about some of my most recent acquisitions from the Witchweb. I sometimes deal in darker themed antiquities, shall we say?"

"You buy and sell black witch stuff, and she wanted to blackmail you so your family or the SPAFS admin wouldn't find out?"

A rusty laugh broke out from the man. "That's the problem. She didn't do her research. My name descends not only from Merlin but Morgan Le Fay as well." He paused and waited for Xandie's reaction. "That's right. You grew up human, didn't you?"

Said like an insult with a heavy dose of pity. Xandie forced herself to play nice. Pasting a saccharine sweet smile on, she agreed. "I did, but don't worry, the Harrows and the library dealt with that ignorance."

"Most of the Harrows are unremarkable, but Elspeth is impressive enough to carry them all. And what supernatural hasn't consulted the Great Library of Alexandria?"

Xandie prodded the human-hating bigot. "The blackmail?"

"She'd imagined I'd want to keep my dark magic predilections quiet. But my family and I couldn't care less. In fact, I'm the most easy-going of my family line. As for SPAFS, while I'm doing a favor for the organizers, my predilections are irrelevant. I told that LaRue creature the same thing. One must have subtlety when conducting the art of blackmail and do one's research. She didn't take it well." He snickered for a moment. "She was quite desperate for money. Something to do with gambling. I saw her that last day, positively gloating over some big scheme coming to fruition."

"Maybe a blackmail plot came through?"

"*Quite.* I thought I'd make myself useful and impart some of my knowledge to you."

"Nice of you." This creepy, uptight guy was the most easy-going of his family? Xandie shuddered mentally, where the predator couldn't pick up a weakness.

"Not really. Now, the library itself owes me a favor. Or at least, a consideration." Myrddin stood and tipped an imaginary hat.

"Hang on a second. Did you see Lorelei talking to anyone the day she died?"

"Oh, she talked to quite a few people that day. But her secret meeting with the Kitsune man looked to be the most interesting."

"One other thing—this favor you were doing SPAFS?"

"One of their usual judges was sick. I know one of the backers and offered to step in. There are a few good suppliers around here that only work face-to-face. Our needs dovetailed."

Xandie groaned. "Let me guess, Elspeth Harrow?"

"Your grandmother works only by referral and was one of my stops. It was well-planned, although all the squabbling beforehand made me almost reconsider my position."

"Squabbling?"

"Contract negotiation between SPAFS and Malachi Mede. He had advice from someone about adding a special clause in and wouldn't sign until it was added."

Clause. That spelled clue to Xandie. "Any idea what it was?"

Myrddin shrugged. "No. But it would be on his copy of the contract. All I know is that he spoke to a resort property consultant who advised him to add it. Caused SPAFS no end of grief, but they agreed to it in the end. They had very little choice at the last minute."

"Had SPAFS had any trouble with blackmailers?"

"Not that I know of. But I did hear through the grapevine there have been ASP sightings in the Point Muse surroundings. The news might interest you and the library, considering your connection to them. Now good day, Ms. Meyers." Myrddin retreated from the bakery as Lila poked her head out of the kitchen.

"Freak show gone?"

Xandie ignored Lila and pondered the said freaky man's words. Kitsune could only mean one person. Shan. And Lorelei had met with him on the day she died. *Interesting.* What was the bet that Shan had been the property consultant who wanted the clause added?

Shot him right to the top of the suspect list. At least for now. Then Myrrdin's last warning about ASP. Maybe that prickling on her nape, and the feeling of being watched, wasn't Harrow paranoia. As Elspeth would say, it wasn't paranoia if they were out to get you. Elspeth still refused to talk about her eldest daughter, but when it came down to it, none of the Harrows would let ASP hurt Xandie or her missing mom.

"Earth to Xandie. Come in. You with me?"

"Working the puzzle pieces out. Seeing what fits in my mind."

"And?"

"And that polite Mr. Shan, Japanese Kitsune and resort developer extraordinaire, is in it up to his furry little ears."

Lila clapped her hands. "Woot. We have a suspect."

Xandie agreed with a nod. "We have a suspect."

Lila high-fived her. "About damn time. Normally you're quicker than that."

"It's not like I'm an expert! I'm still learning the murder investigation ropes." Xandie stood and stretched. "Got anything planned tonight? Fancy a little breaking and entering?"

"I wish." Lila made a face. "Aggie trapped me into providing refreshments for the citizen watch group she runs tonight. No chance of felonies when the police dispatcher has eyes on you."

"Your loss." Xandie stuck her tongue out and headed for the door.

"Need a ride?"

"In your bakery deathtrap van? No thanks. I'll have a leisurely stroll home. Hey, Lila?"

"Yes, dearest cousin who hasn't annoyed me yet today?"

"Watch yourself and the rest of the family, okay?"

"What's Elspeth done now?"

"That man, Myrddin? Told me ASP has been seen in town."

Lila gathered a few plates off an empty table. "Don't worry your geeky little head about it. We Harrows take care of each other. ASP won't dare come near Elspeth. Who knows how many of them she's already buried out the back of Harrow House. You focus on solving the murders or you'll deal with Elspeth instead, and she's far worse."

Relieved at passing her message on, even if it was ignored, Xandie poked her tongue out at her cousin again and then stepped out onto Main Street. The town had been busy since SPAFS had come. A little tourist dollar in the coffers was a wonderful thing.

Even if it did bring murder to Point Muse. Xandie ambled past a couple of stores with opening soon signs. The last few months had seen new people settle into town, a gypsy being one of them. Zelda was planning to open a fortune telling and occult shop in the next few months. At least some Harrows were excited about it, but Elspeth pooh-poohed the idea. Nothing visible on a shelf was worth buying.

"Well, well. Look who we have here?" A short, older man with a yellowed beard stepped in front of Xandie, barring her way.

This is the same guy who'd scared Amity. The bookie. Xandie smiled sweetly. When in doubt, go on the charm offensive. "Hi. Nice to see the SPAFS crowd patronizing Point Muse." Xandie placed a hand on his arm and continued, "It's people like you who keep Point Muse afloat. Thank you from the bottom of Point Muse's heart."

The older man took a step back, out of range of Xandie's hand. "Yeah, I'm not part of that animal loving crowd."

Xandie pretended to be confused. "But I saw you there with Amity. I assumed, I guess."

"Well, you know what they say about assuming things." He nodded at Xandie.

She blinked her eyes rapidly. "Why, no, I don't.

What does it mean?"

Yellow beard deflated and muttered, "Never mind. I'm here to give

you a warning."

Xandie gasped, hand to her mouth. She fought off a snorting laugh. "Did I forget to pay the parking fine? I swear I meant to."

"What? No. I mean..." He stumbled to a halt before taking a deep breath and plowing on, "Stay out of the LaRue investigation. Or you'll regret it." He eyed Xandie. "You understand me?"

Xandie trilled a fake laugh. "You must have me confused with someone else. I'm not involved in any police work. Just a meek librarian here." Xandie wiggled her fingers in a hello to the yellow bearded man.

He rubbed his sweating forehead and grimaced. "I'm passing a message along, then I'm leaving town. Too hot here right now and it's more profitable to stay away."

"Oh, you poor man. Hot weather is a trial for those who are delicate." Xandie pointed to his head. "Keep an eye on that headache. It could be an aneurysm."

"It's not an aneurysm." He shouted the last word and then visibly calmed himself. "For your own good. Stay out of it. You don't want to end up like LaRue."

"You mean dead because she blackmailed the wrong person?"

Yellow beard looked surprised. "You know about that? There must be more to you than the ditzy librarian schtick. Yeah, she had a few schemes going. She needed the money to pay off her gambling debts." He shook his head. "The lady loved the racing corns but had terrible taste. She was always broke but good at threatening people. I figured that's what killed her. But around here, I guess gambling is a popular affliction."

Xandie cocked her head. "Because other people in Point Muse owe you money?"

The man nodded but then froze.

"Is this gentleman bothering you, Ms. Meyers?" The Kitsune, Shan, loomed behind Xandie.

Suppressing the urge to curse his timing, Xandie shook her head. "Not at all. His face was red and sweaty. So, I thought the heat had affected him."

Shan perused the graying sky. "Seems the heat has gone out of the sun for a while. I'm sure the gentleman will be fine and needs to get along?" Shan posed the question to yellow beard with a lift of an eyebrow.

The bookie nodded vigorously. "Yes sir, Mr. Shan, I do. Thanks for your concern." He stared at Xandie for a few seconds. "Remember what I said, Miss. Look after yourself." He nodded and scuttled across the street and disappeared around the corner.

"You need to be more careful, Ms. Meyers. Accosting strange dwarfs in the street isn't the best strategy for a long-term life."

Dwarf? Explained his short stature and love of gold. "Is that a threat, Mr. Shan?"

"No threat."

"Well then, if that's the case, I have places to be." Xandie sashayed off, feeling smug as she gave Shan the slip.

"It's an observation, but maybe you should listen to the little bookie," Shan called out behind Xandie's back.

The things one learned when warned off by a bookie dwarf. She'd lay bets herself that Shan had paid the bookie to get out of town by the way the little man had frozen when the Kitsune had spoken. Not to mention he'd known the dwarf was a bookie. Things were getting interesting. Xandie continued on home to the relative safety of the library.

So many things to do. Hopefully, none of which included finding another body.

TWELVE

"Are you sure we won't get caught? Because I don't need to add breaking and entering to my growing list of felonies, niece." Amelia passed Xandie a small colorful mechanical bug.

"I asked for a flashlight, Aunt Amelia."

"Tap the bug once to turn on, twice to turn off. It's one of Elspeth's monstrous experiments with science and magic." Amelia frowned. "It's unnatural but works well."

Xandie tapped the bug, and a small glowing amber light illuminated the old-fashioned brass lock she was attempting to pick. "Surely a flashlight would have been easier?"

Amelia shrugged. "Where's the devious Harrow

detail in that? This way it looks like a kid's gadget if we get caught. Instead of a conspicuous and suspicious flashlight." Amelia peered at the lock. "Are you sure you know how to pick it?"

"The library found me a book on how to pick a cursed lock. I'm hoping the mechanics are the same for a normal one."

"Hoping. *Great.*" Amelia sat, her back against the door.

"Unless you have a skeleton key or a spell to open it, this is the only idea I've got to get into Mede's office." Xandie had cut a piece of wire from one of her coat hangers. Now she fashioned it into a lock-picking shape by creating a ninety-degree angle at one end. "I'm doing everything the book said to do, except getting it blessed by a holy man. I'm hoping it will get us into the office." Xandie slipped the wire into the keyhole. She pushed a little farther until the wire hit something. Taking a deep breath, Xandie twisted the wire.

Supposedly if she felt the lock bolt move, she was successful. No movement. Xandie removed the wire from the lock and wiped her hands on her black jeans. This was harder than the book had made it seem. She tried again, but no matter what Xandie did, nothing worked. No movement, no click, no open door. Xandie sat back on her heels and growled.

"This might work." A white, hand-carved key dangled in front of Xandie.

Xandie grabbed the key; it might fit the lock. She squinted from the key up to the person who dangled it in front of her. Her grandmother, Elspeth, wearing long, black pants, a long-sleeved black shirt, and a dark scarf wound around her head. She even had black camouflage paint on her face. Xandie groaned. "Why am I not surprised you had a key? And why are you dressed like an elderly ninja?"

Elspeth sniffed. "*First off*, I am ashamed any granddaughter of mine couldn't invite me to a break and enter. *Second,* these are my felony clothing and *third,* your Aunt Amelia squealed like a hexed rat."

"Is there no secrecy between Harrows?" Xandie whined. She stared at the key. Someone had carved white striations out of the material. Rounded at one end and curved at the other, the key had a skinny shaft connecting the two ends. "How'd you get a key to Mede's office?"

Elspeth smirked. "I didn't. I made this one and added a few spell touches to it."

Xandie peered at it. Something about the spindly

whitish-gray key freaked her out. She couldn't quite work out what. "What is it? What's it made out of?"

"It's a skeleton key. Literally made from human bone. Auntie Rose would have been delighted to know she was breaking and entering."

Oh God. Elspeth had dug up a dead aunt and carved the key out of her bones. Xandie dropped the key onto the floor and gagged. Her grandmother was a grave robber. *Oh, the shame.*

Elspeth tsked and picked up the key. "Grow a Harrow spine, girl. My aunt Rose lost a finger to a troll. They sent it back with an apology, but by that time, she'd grown another one with the help of a frogspawn potion. She gave this one to me to practice on." Elspeth gave a shimmy and unlocked the door. "Technically it's called a bit and barrel key, but I prefer skeleton key."

"Still not touching it." Xandie pointed at Amelia as she crept into the room behind Elspeth. "Not finished with you either, Aunt. No one likes a rat."

"When it comes to my mother, it's every witch for herself." Amelia rolled her eyes.

"Can we focus, children? Let's get to it. I don't need any more charges on my rap sheet, so I don't plan to get caught." Elspeth headed for a cabinet and started leafing through the files. "Now what is it you need, Xandie?"

Xandie mouthed *rap sheet* at Amelia, but she shook her head. Xandie cleared her throat. "We're after financial papers relating to SPAFS, anything to do with Shan resort group or the Medes' finances."

"Hop to it, jailbait. This is your rodeo." Elspeth toasted Amelia with a hip flask after deserting the filing cabinet.

"Give it up, Mother. Everyone in town knows that's iced tea in there."

"Is it, Amelia?" Elspeth drawled. "If everyone says so, it must be right." She drank deep, coughed, and then thumped her chest. "Yep, damn good iced tea. Carry on, girlies, carry on."

Ignoring her grandmother's antics, Xandie peered around the office. Malachi Mede was the complete opposite of Lorelei LaRue, a neat freak instead of a slob. Everything was color coordinated and lined up like little stationary soldiers. Xandie peered at the desk but didn't bother touching anything. Mede would know if anything was moved, and there were no personal papers or bank finance statements littering the surface. She tugged on the desk drawers, but they were all locked. "Would Aunt Rose's finger work on desk drawers too?"

"No point. He might lock it, but no one worth an ounce of brains would leave secret goodies in their drawers."

Not going there. Xandie wandered around the office. Amelia flicked through filing cabinets and Elspeth chugged on her flask.

"Nothing here, Xandie. Personal files, orders, schedules, nothing about finances." Amelia made a face and slammed the file drawer shut before moving to another.

Xandie shook her head. The difference between the everyday human world and the supernatural Point Muse one was more than obvious in this office. No computer sitting on the desk. Technology didn't work reliably when around supernaturals and ley lines.

"This is a bust. Let's skedaddle before the fuzz catches us." Elspeth hid her hip flask away.

"Hang on." Xandie spun around. Something about this room felt off. She ran her hand along a wall hung with pictures, paintings, and decorated shelving. She stopped in front of an arched built-in bookcase. "Now, like in those old detective novels you like, Elspeth, what's the bet this is a false bookcase with something behind it?"

Elspeth chortled. "I told you those books would come in handy. Push it, Xandie girl."

"You're both crazy. Trust me, Xandie, insanity is not the trait you want to take away from Harrow blood."

"You know what, Aunt Amelia? Can't hurt to try." Xandie pressed against the shelves, but they refused to move. Undaunted, she ran her hands around the edge of the bookcase and over the shelves. Nestled right on the back edge of a shelf was a raised bump. Xandie pressed it down, and the bookcase swung back a few inches.

"I take back everything I said." Amelia crowded behind Xandie with Elspeth following on their heels.

Xandie stepped through the opening. It was a tiny area, enough room so her aunt and grandmother could stand side-by-side but that was all. Lengthwise, it was a compact closet space that only went a few feet back. Every available wall had a shelf fixed to it and was crammed with boxes. "Well, well. Organization gone mad." Xandie peered into a box but could barely see anything in the dark.

"This might help." Elspeth grabbed a string hanging from the ceiling and tugged. A small bare globe flared to life, illuminating the room and filling the space with a buzzing, electrical sound.

"Okay, we're looking for anything to do with SPAFS, Mede's finances, and anything to do with the Shan resort properties. Go, Harrows." Xandie took the end of the shelves facing the door. Elspeth took one side and Amelia the other.

Thank God Mede was anal and labeled everything. Each box had a title ranging from products to schedules. Xandie ran her finger along the shelves, but most of the boxes on the top few shelves were all about ordering supplies. Xandie read the titles along the bottom shelf.

"I got financials." Elspeth waved the bank statement in the air.

"And I have betting slips," Amelia joined in.

"I have nada, zip, zero." Xandie sighed and leaned her head against a shelf. She peered down at her feet. She needed to find that pet show contract, but so far nothing on the shelves was remotely close. As she moved away from the shelves, a wedge of creamy white paper stuck under a box caught her eye.

Interesting. Mede was organized to a demonic degree. *So why loose papers?* Xandie tugged the papers free and scanned them. *Bingo.* The Supernatural Pet and Familiar Show contract. The first few pages talked about the event, laid out basic stages of the show, venue rental fees, services provided by the resort venue. Setting up of marquees, provision of shipping and minimum food and beverage needs. Requirements for the animals, grooming, rest, safety, and direction of the competing rings and arenas for each stage were also listed.

Xandie skipped to the back of the contract, where an SPAFS appointed organizer had signed. Under Malachi Mede's name was an addendum to the contract. The resort would charge a substantial fee if SPAFS were to cancel the event. A policy that activated if the event was canceled after the start date. One hundred percent refund of all fees and expenses incurred by the venue plus a penalty fee of fifty percent of the final stated venue cost.

"Wow, Mede stands to gain if they cancel the event." And look who witnessed the contract. *Naruto Shan.*

"And the Mede family needs the cash." Elspeth tapped the paper she was holding with an iridescent painted talon. "Says here the company is running on fumes. A resort built in Point Muse was expensive because of the ley lines. They had to hire experts and shore up wards and foundations of the building to combat any ley line movement or surges. That energy work is highly specific, and anyone who practices it charges through the nose."

Amelia flashed her own pile of yellow slips. "Then there are these. Mostly from the same racetrack, the major one Lorelei gambled at. And all in Hannah Mede's name." Amelia shook her head. "She was quiet and hard-working when she worked for me. I can't believe she's a racing corn addict."

"Happens to the best of us. You should see High Priestess Lilith now. She's living on the streets in Boston. Complete mess." Elspeth nodded in agreement. "Besides, it's always the quiet ones."

"What about Shan? Did we find anything on him?"

Both Elspeth and Amelia shook their heads.

"Slippery fox likes to keep his name out of things, I think." Xandie put the papers back in the same place she found them and stood. "Right, put everything back. And be careful, or Mede might notice something's out of place. Tomorrow, I'll track Hannah down and ask her what's going on."

The women replaced the papers and filed out. Xandie pushed the bookcase back into place, and Elspeth locked the door with Rose's finger.

Hannah Mede was a gambling addict, and her resort had almost bankrupted what was left of the

Mede fortune. Was Hannah engineering her own accidents to get SPAFS to cancel and pay them? Whatever was happening was a lot more complicated than a killer on a bloody eliminate-the-competition killing spree.

Why couldn't life in Point Muse be a little more cadaver free?

THIRTEEN

"You need to tell the truth. We're trying to help." Xandie reached out and grabbed Hannah's hand, giving it a squeeze. She'd lain awake for hours last night going over every tragic moment so far. Every aspect, every piece of information learned and gathered. Everything pointed to Hannah being the culprit. But she couldn't see either of the Medes being cold-blooded killers. *Shan, on the other hand...*

Hannah shook off Xandie's touch and glared at both her and Lila. "I keep telling you. I had nothing to do with the murders. And I've never gambled in my life." Hannah paused for a moment. "Now you mention it? Scientifically? I could craft a mathematical equation that might help with analyzing and picking a winner."

"Focus, Mede. Geez, you can't separate the geek from the girl, can you?"

Hannah glowered at Lila. "I. Am. Not. A. Geek. It was an idea."

Xandie made a timeout with her hands. "No need to name call. We found evidence of betting slips in your name, and according to your financials, unless SPAFS cancels, or you sell your resort to Shan, you're running on empty."

Hannah shook her head. "Not possible. Malachi would tell me if we were in dire trouble. Yes, I wanted the resort here, but not if it'd bankrupt us."

Lila paced from one side of Hannah's office to the other. "What about Shan? What do you know about him? What's his deal with the resort?"

"Only that he's been hanging around a lot. He advised Malachi on the SPAFS contract and other business things. He's been helpful, but he just won't go away. Every time I turn around, he's always there, watching me."

"He's protecting you," Xandie offered, not believing her own words. Shan had a reason for attaching himself to Hannah, but it wasn't protection.

Hannah snorted. "I may look blonde and fragile,

but the one thing Point Muse taught me was look pretty, act deadly. As long as you don't get caught. It's all unicorns and magic rainbows."

"Cynical, but appropriate for Point Muse," Lila offered.

"Heard anything about Shan buying your resort?"

Hannah shook her head again. "Not a thing. And with all the issues and accidents around this place, I'd happily sell to get away."

"Maybe that's the plan?" Xandie wondered aloud.

Lila tapped a finger on the window behind Hannah's desk. "You think that's it? Force Hannah to sell because of bad luck? It stinks like motivation to me."

"It's working." Hannah made a face. "Galls me to slink out of town with my figurative tail between my legs, but I've had enough of this damn town *and* the resort."

"Shan has an ulterior motive, and this could be it. He's ruthless enough to be a killer, both financially and physically."

"Well, Xandie, you better develop that killer instinct yourself." Lila tapped the window again.

Xandie closed her eyes. *Please don't let it be another dead body.*

"Elspeth, Winifred, and Colin are on the warpath, heading this way."

"Almost as bad," Xandie mumbled to herself.

"Slide out the back way, through the kitchen. You should be able to get to the grooming tent before they circle back around and catch you," Hannah said with a grin. "Pretend you've been there the whole time and bluff it out. They won't be able to say anything."

Lila whistled in surprise. "Who'd have thought quiet, mousey Hannah would be so devious?"

"Side effect of working with Harrows."

"Well, this little librarian is off to avoid said Harrows." Xandie risked a glance out the window. Elspeth *was* on the pet show warpath if that frown she was wearing was any indicator. *Ducking and hiding it is.* With a wave to Lila and Hannah, Xandie crept out the door and headed for the grooming tent. As she got closer, muffled voices drew her attention.

"Do you think you'll get away with it? Someone will notice."

"Who, George? Sorry, should I call you Giorgio?" Lulu sneered at her ex-husband.

Lulu and George Moon fighting? *Time to snoop.* Xandie slowed her pace and moved out of sight, pretending to tie her sneakers while she eavesdropped on the squabbling exes.

"Cut the crap, Lulu. I've been an idiot. Between LaRue and the name change, everyone's laughing at me. But I've never seen you so obsessed that you're willing to cross so many lines."

Lulu grated out a rusty laugh. "What would you know about me lately, George? You're the one who left, remember?"

"And I've regretted it ever since. I was an idiot to think LaRue would help me. But you must realize—"

"What? That you left me because she offered that damn potion to make your hair grow? Dangled it in front of you like a carrot. You would've done anything she wanted."

"You don't understand," George wailed. "Baldness in a man is an evil curse. I wanted my masculinity back, my flowing locks."

"Buy a wig. You're sixty years old. Act your age," Lulu hissed back at him.

Sixty years old? George looked at the most in his forties. Supernaturals definitely aged slower than humans. She could barely comprehend it.

George changed the subject. "This isn't about me. It's about you. Lulu, you need to stop now before you do something you'll really regret."

"The only thing I regret is not beating that obnoxious pug and not getting rid of you earlier."

Lulu stormed past Xandie and then backtracked to stand in front of her. "What a surprise. Someone eavesdropping. You going to blackmail me too? Seems to be a favorite sport around here."

Xandie straightened from her crouch. "Nope, no blackmailing here. Just tying loose laces."

Lulu curled her top lip. "You and your pug disgust me. My Princess is worth a hundred of that dog. I'll show you. I'll show you all what she can do. Whatever the cost." Lulu spat at the ground where Xandie stood and then stormed off.

"Okay, that's just plain gross, particularly coming from a woman. Sometimes Colin disgusts me too, what with all that farting and the belching, but I think Lulu has him beat."

"I'm sorry, Ms. Meyers. Lulu is under a lot of pressure." George Moon stood nearby, wringing his hands, delicate wispy blond hair smoothed over a balding skull.

"She's sure wound tight, but she shouldn't worry. Her rabbit is miles ahead in the rankings now."

"Lulu's always been competitive, but LaRue really pushed her buttons."

"You mean since you left her for Lorelei?"

George sighed. "The biggest mistake of my life. Lorelei offered to supply me with a hair potion and her condition was that I leave Lulu." He looked down at his feet and shuffled a little before meeting Xandie's gaze. "I'm ashamed to admit I agreed. Once she had a hold over me, she started milking me for cash. I never even saw the potion, and I lost Lulu forever."

"What has Lulu done that crosses a line?"

"Her Princess gets anxious before she competes. Lulu's helping her to deal with it...*medicinally*. I told her she's obsessed, and she'll hurt Princess, but Lulu won't listen to me anymore." He slumped, dejected. "Why should she after what I've done? But I've scratched Lucifer, my golden goose. Your pug and Lulu's rabbit are now the last competitors in the running. I hope she survives this fiasco and I can convince her to give me a second chance." George nodded to Xandie and shuffled off, a broken man.

Xandie shook her head. The pet show circuit was a regular soap opera. Villains, blackmail, affairs, and murder. A writer could make a financial killing with these storylines.

"Well, if it isn't the prodigal granddaughter lurking outside the grooming tent. We're dishonored by your presence." Elspeth Harrow stood there, tapping her pointed black boot on the muddy ground.

Xandie took in the sartorial cliché her grandmother was currently sporting. A thick burgundy velvet cloak with a voluminous hood landed midcalf. Glittering rings in a variety of gaudy colors adorned Elspeth's fingers and black-and-white striped stockings with sharp pointed leather ankle boots completed the witchy picture. "Which wicked witch are you?"

From the depths of the hood, Elspeth intoned. "One you've never encountered before, librarian. Cross me and I will hex your laces so you always trip."

Family... "Okay, what did I do now?"

Elspeth shoved the hood back, revealing today's neon green wig. "Talent practice. Remember? Except Xandie Meyers didn't show because she's consumed with catlike curiosity about death, which will probably get her offed someday." Elspeth wound down with a huff.

"Your lung capacity for an older witch is impressive." Xandie sighed. Getting mouthy with Elspeth never worked, but cowardly crawling did. "I'm sorry, my wise and talented grandmother. You're right. I was occupied. But I'm here now, so what do you want me to do?"

Mollified, Elspeth sniffed. "That's more the attitude. This is a team, Xandie. Everyone pulls their weight."

"How's the detecting going, kiddo? Lassoed any suspects yet?" Colin climbed out from underneath Elspeth's cloak and scratched behind his ear with a rear leg, dislodging his black top hat.

"Colin, be careful you don't get your costume dirty." Elspeth chided the pug and grabbed his hat from the ground, dusting it off.

Colin and a black top hat and tie did not bode well for the talent stage. Xandie shuddered to think what Elspeth had picked, considering her crazed choices of disguise. "I'm getting there. I've got a suspect in mind, and I'm sure I know who turned Lorelei LaRue to stone."

"Progress, kid. Nothing to sneeze at." Colin let out a belch and adjusted his bowtie with a paw.

Winifred jogged up, chest heaving as she gasped out her news. "Have you heard? A basilisk has been sighted near Point Muse Academy. Police and the shifters organized a hunting party. The cops are press-ganging all creature experts into the hunt. Did you want me to run the practice while you speak to the chief, Mother?"

Elspeth flipped the hood back over her head and mumbled something noncommittal.

When did her blunt, devious grandmother suddenly become evasive? "Elspeth? Why would the chief want to speak to you? What have you done?"

"I have no idea. I'm innocent. Why does everyone always blame me?" Elspeth's voice squeaked as she played the persecuted witch in a superb performance.

Winifred glanced between Xandie and her mother. "Mom's an expert on basilisk control and care. She's the only licensed operator in the district besides Amelia. Basilisks are such dangerous animals certified handlers must own or treat them. And the only way is to use control magic through a specially made amulet. Elspeth's the best there is." Winifred beamed at her mother.

"Elspeth Harrow. What have you done?" Xandie glared at her grandmother. If the elder witch was such an expert, she would have known from the beginning what killed LaRue. And she hadn't said a word. *To anyone.*

"Ratted out by my own daughter. It's your

father's blood getting back at me." Elspeth sighed and then gave in. "I may have had an order for a basilisk control collar from a not so savory contact."

Damn her grandmother and her black-market shady connections. "And?"

"I only work through referrals but..." Elspeth cleared her throat. "Fresh cash was needed for a certain project, and I thought it wouldn't matter this once to break my rules."

"We need the name of the person who requested that collar. They could be our mastermind behind these killings."

Elspeth winced. "About that... The referral was by a third party Witchweb broker. I've no clue who was the eventual recipient."

Xandie waved her hands in the air. "Why do I feel like I'm the only adult here? Find me that name ASAP, Elspeth Harrow."

"Or what?" Elspeth sounded interested in Xandie's answer.

"I'll ask Pastor Ezekiel to drop off a heavenly choir at your door and let them loose with their angelic trumpets every morning at dawn. You'll never get any sleep."

Elspeth gasped. "You'd do that to your poor grandmother? Xandie Meyers, I'm proud of you."

Elspeth shook as she forced back fake tears. "Finally, one of my grandchildren is resorting to the threat of torture. This is my proudest moment." She held a hand to her heart.

Winifred took one look at Xandie's exasperated face and steered her mother away while still clutching Colin. "Mom, why don't you head back to Harrow House to research, and I'll help Xandie and Colin practice."

Elspeth wiped away a tear and agreed, yelling over her shoulder as she went, "You've always been my favorite. It's the human blood that adds deviousness to the mix. I'm sure of it."

Xandie rubbed her forehead as her grandmother disappeared into the distance.

"Soon as I met that dame, I knew she'd give someone a brain tumor," Colin offered from his inappropriate perch next to Winifred's chest.

"I do not have a *tumor*," Xandie yelled the last word, her patience tested by Harrow deviousness and a mouthy pug. *Déjà vu*. She'd confused the bookie dwarf with the same argument. Now she knew how frustrated that poor dwarf must have felt.

Xandie needed to find the killer as soon as possible and then a long grandmother-free vacation was in her cards. She needed Elspeth, SPAFS, and the killer to cooperate...

Some days she could see why her mother had married her no-nonsense, stable father.

Point Muse plus Harrow blood always equaled chaos and mayhem.

FOURTEEN

"I'll never be able to wipe this from my memory. It's burned there forever," Xandie wailed, trying to cover her eyes.

"He's a star, isn't he? Blazing too bright for us to stare at. We must only worship from afar," Winifred gushed.

"Like I said, doll-face. If you've got it, flaunt it." Colin waggled his short curly tail and twirled a small silver baton on his little nose.

The routine Elspeth had planned and choreographed was the secret weapon to slaughter the competition. The same competition composed of only one other animal. Princess, the purple sparkle Angora rabbit. When George Moon scratched his goose, it'd only left two competitors to fight it out.

Elspeth had designed a special routine that would shoot them up to equal first place. A dance routine that seemed to be part baton twirling, part stripper. You'd never be closer to experiencing torture than if you'd watched a talking pug grind his way through a jazz hands tune.

"This is in the bag, baby. No rabbit's gonna out-swivel me." Colin rolled his hips and back end at Xandie, while still balancing his baton.

"Three hours. Three hours of a blinding headache and a grinding pug. What did I do to deserve this?" Xandie mumbled to herself. This was Elspeth's bad karma rebounding onto her. Life wasn't fair.

"Cheer up. I'm here with liquid refreshment." Lila grinned and waggled a takeaway cup from her bakery under Xandie's nose.

"I don't think there's enough chocolate in Point Muse to deal with this visual atrocity." Xandie pointed a finger at Colin's gyrations.

"That's why I added a shot of Witchshine to it. Enjoy." Lila beamed and waggled the cup again at Xandie until she grabbed it and swigged a mouthful.

Shivering as the warm liquid burnt its way down, Xandie took another small mouthful before placing it on the table out of reach. She needed all her faculties sharp if she wanted to survive a killer *and* her grandmother.

"Elspeth strikes again?" Lila nodded at Colin.

"I don't know whether to laugh, cry, or run away," Xandie admitted.

"Probably all three. At least it'll be over soon. For us, anyway. You might have to deal with the fallout for a while longer."

"Our grandmother holding a grudge is the least of my worries. I have a nasty feeling we're going to see more bodies. I can't stop this killer."

"Elspeth's going through her records and applying pressure on her Witchweb broker for a name, but it's going to take a while."

"Time we don't have." Xandie picked her cup up again and cradled it, lost in thought. Shan was behind all the bodies and the accidents centered on Hannah. She was sure of it. He seemed the most likely suspect right now. But how could she prove it? She needed to bait Shan out into the open and get a confession. Then, bam, lower the Elspeth boom on him.

"Elspeth boom?" Lila shot a wide-eyed glance at her cousin. "Maybe you should put your drink down for now. I think it's gone to your head." Lila grabbed the doctored hot chocolate and placed it out of reach.

Whoops. Those last few words must've been out loud. "Thinking ahead to when I take our killer down."

"And Elspeth's your muscle?"

Xandie rolled her eyes. "Sadly, yes. No way do I want Chief Braun sweeping in and saving the day and the heroine."

"You are definitely a Harrow. The way you hold grudges is epic."

Xandie jutted her chin out. "He's an annoying pain in my…"

"Five minutes to talent stage." Winifred tapped her watch. "Let's get our star out there and ready to go."

Xandie frowned. Who'd be more traumatized after this? *Me or the judges?* At least Davros had convinced Moonshadow to stay. She'd seen him mumbling to himself behind the makeshift stage earlier. Penny pincher SPAFS must've coughed up a little more cash for the flight risk judge.

***

"Ta da," Colin sang as he wiggled his back and pranced around the makeshift stage.

Xandie covered her face with sweaty palms as

the pug passed wind in excitement. The front row occupants jerked back and covered their noses. She'd warned against that last cream cheese and red pepper canape, but when it came to food, Colin was all stomach.

Alex Pennywort, host of the show, coughed and stepped forward, his eyes watering. "Thank you, Colin the pug for your memorable performance. Now we'd like to call Princess, handled by Lulu Moon, to the stage." Alex led the applause, which died down as no one appeared.

"Ms. Moon?" he called again and waited for a few moments more. "I'm sorry, but as per our guidelines, the competitor and handler must be on the stage ready to perform within a five-minute interval or forfeit that stage." Pennywort paused again, but there was no sign of Lulu and her purple rabbit.

Pennywort took a breath and declared, "With no other choice, because of competitor withdrawals and the non-attendance of Princess, I declare Colin the pug the winner of the talent contest. I will announce final rankings at the last stage, which is a static stack for five minutes in front of the judges." Pennywort nodded to a cavorting Colin. "Congratulations again, Colin."

Colin bopped over to Xandie, who stood at the

end of the makeshift stage. "What did I tell you, doll-face? Colin's got the moves."

"You won by default because everyone else dropped out and the rabbit didn't show."

Colin sneezed a goblet of green snot in Xandie's direction. "Still counts, toots. Equal first, wahoo."

The pug would never come down from this high. They'd have to widen the doorways at Harrow House to accommodate his ego.

"Can't bring me down, chickie." Colin wiped a fake tear away with a paw. "Elspeth would be proud."

God save me from the dramatics of a hyperactive pug.

"My precious Colin. Mother will be excited." Winifred rushed in, and crouched next to Colin, covering his head in kisses. "Who's a talented boy?"

Colin belched a cream cheese and red pepper cloud into Winifred's face, causing her to retch. "Told you I had it handled. You call in a pro when you need the job done right."

Waving a hand at the belch cloud in front of her, Winifred grabbed Colin and stood, cooing at him until Xandie cleared her throat.

"Should we tell Elspeth about Colin's default win?"

Winifred waved off Xandie's suggestion. "Oh, she'll have scried it out already. She's preparing her victory speech for the competition."

"Elspeth's avoiding me, isn't she?" Otherwise her grandmother would have been down here in disguise, tormenting her.

"Your grandmother had a minor difficulty tracking the name of the person you wanted, but she's still digging." Winifred frowned as she sniffed Colin's coat. "What's that stink?"

"Colin dived into the prawn cocktail at lunch. The seafood odor might have stuck."

Winifred shook her head. "No. That's not appropriate for our winner. He needs to smell of victory, not fish. There's a spray bottle of eau de Elspeth in the grooming tent. Could you fetch it please, Xandie?"

"Sure, back to that damn tent. That's what I'm here for." Xandie stomped off, mumbling, "Fetch and carry for an oversexed crime against nature. That's what my job's down to." She ducked into the grooming tent and sagged. Thankfully, the show was almost over. Xandie couldn't wait for life to get back to normal...well, as normal as it could be in Point Muse.

Xandie rummaged through Colin's grooming

tools and sighed as Elspeth's perfumed spray bottle failed to appear. "What a surprise. Nothing is going right today." Giving up, she checked Amity's treatment room in the hopes of finding something to combat Colin's fishy stench. She flicked the door flap open and headed for a set of makeshift cupboards. "There has to be something here that might work." Reading the names on the different colored bottles as she searched, Xandie crowed when she came across one marked *stench away*. "Eureka, Colin stink is a thing of the past." She spun and tripped over a pill bottle laying open on the floor. Her arms flayed in the air, and she grabbed onto Amity's treatment table in the middle of the room. A squeak slipped from Xandie as she realized what was behind the table. Lulu Moon's prone body laid out on the floor, with Princess in a cage next to her.

Dumping Colin's stench bottle on the table, Xandie kneeled to take her pulse. Nothing. Lulu Moon was stone cold dead with a bunch of pills ringing her body. Xandie moved back. The flap of the treatment room lifted, and Winifred poked her head in.

"Don't worry about the scent bottle. I found ours in my handbag." Winifred frowned at Xandie's white-as-a-ghost complexion. "What's wrong, sweetie?"

"I found Lulu and Princess." Xandie pointed a trembling finger behind her. "You need to call Braun. We have another body."

Winifred jerked back, hand to her mouth, before jogging away as fast as her plump body would allow.

"Poor Princess." Xandie took a step toward the cage to check on the rabbit, but the animal calmly chewed on her carrot. She stepped back and stood on the empty pill bottle again. Bending down, she used an abandoned comb to nudge it around so she could read the sticker on the side of the container. The last thing Xandie needed was to add her fingerprints into the mix.

She squinted. "Kava, chamomile, and vitamin b complex. Once a day for anxiety. Doctor Amelia Harrow, Harrow Vet Clinic and Holistic Healing, Point Muse." *Holy rabbit nerves.* Her aunt Amelia had prescribed antianxiety tablets for Princess. The same date Velma Mystic had died. Princess must've been the emergency patient Amelia had worked on that night. And now, Lulu lay dead with Amelia's pills all around her. This wouldn't end well.

"Seriously, Meyers. You have a death addiction."

The not-so-dulcet tones of Police Chief Zachary

Braun grated on Xandie's last nerve. She glared at the broad-shouldered policeman and ignored the way his floppy, sandy brown hair hung over deep blue eyes. "Not death addicted. Catalyst, remember? Not my choice to find another body."

Braun crouched down to take Lulu's pulse, but his hand dropped away when he found nothing. "And yet I always seem to find you in the vicinity." He rolled the pill bottle over so he could read the label. "I'm sorry Xandie, but you know what I have to do now."

Xandie slammed her hands on her hips. "You know Amelia isn't the killer."

He straightened and stared at her, remorse oozing out of his every pore. "Too many coincidences are adding up to the fact Amelia's involved. I can't sit on this evidence. I have to arrest her. Get her things together and come down to the station with her. I can at least give you that."

Xandie growled. "This isn't right, Braun."

"Murder never is, Meyers." He turned to call his deputy brothers in but paused without looking at her. "I don't want you investigating, but if someone found evidence to suggest another killer with motive? Well, I'd be able to use that to leverage

Amelia's release." He turned his back to the body and Xandie as his deputies piled in.

Xandie pushed past Zach's brothers. She had an aunt to clear and a killer to stop.

It's time to bring in the big guns.

FIFTEEN

Who'd have thought big guns meant a bottle of her favorite champagne?

"Are you sure you got the spell right?" Xandie shuffled the hexed alcohol behind another bottle on the shelf above the kitchen counter.

"Please, I can follow directions. Besides, Elspeth brewed the honesty curse, mixed in some raw spirits, and added a cloaking agent to disguise the taste before she mixed it into the champagne. It'll work."

Elspeth swore the honesty hex would turn Shan's tongue blue and force him to answer questions. "And Elspeth promised it would work on a Kitsune?"

Lila stared at a spot behind Xandie's shoulder. "Again, yes. No issues. Stop worrying."

Xandie rolled her eyes. "Except for Elspeth, Harrows make terrible liars."

Lila grimaced. "I'm working on the lying thing. Okay, Elspeth is positive it would work on a witch or a human, but she isn't as sure about how the Kitsune's metabolism will interact with the hex. You might not have much time, but it should work."

Xandie groaned. "Just my luck. It's the only plan I have right now."

"Dose him and hope for the best. That's all you can do."

Nodding in agreement, Xandie winced when a tinkle of glass on tile filtered into the kitchen.

Winifred burst through the door, huffing and puffing. "Dear, we've had a slight mishap with a glass of bubbly. Could you bring a mop?" Winifred, without waiting for an answer, charged back out the door.

"Do you regret Elspeth planning a cocktail party at your house yet?" Lila snorted and popped two cheese canapes into her mouth, cheeks bulging like a chipmunk.

Xandie grabbed a mop and a bucket from the cleaning cupboard and shuffled toward the cocktail chaos. "If it gets Shan to divulge his motives and guilt, I'm all for it. As long as there's no vomiting, I'll cope." Xandie ignored Lila's snorting and brandished the mop as she braved the noisy crowd.

"Over here. Yoo-hoo, Alexandra." Dorothy Johnson, elderly witch hairdresser and brand-new judge, hollered away. "Sister had a wee spill of this delicious champagne."

"Don't go too far with your praise. The bubbles are fun, but it ain't a patch on Elspeth's Witchshine." Olive Johnson, Dorothy's sister-in-law, hiccupped, her platinum blonde wig already tilted off-center. The hairdressing duo supplied all the wigs for the township, including Elspeth's psychedelic wigged ensembles.

"Glad you're enjoying the get-together." Xandie mopped up the spill and collected the glass shards in her hand, dropping them into a trashcan placed at the side of the room.

"We were surprised about the last-minute invitation, considering..." Dorothy leaned forward and whispered, "Your Aunt Amelia's unfortunate incarceration."

"Unfortunate? I say about time the Harrows got what they deserved." Madelyn Luna, SPAFS chef and Lila's nemesis, stood swaying, an empty glass in hand.

"Amelia's innocent until proven guilty." Xandie

glared at her cousin Lila's mortal enemy. The chef had cut loose. Gone were the chef hat and jacket, and in their place, she wore a blood red corset top with skinny black jeans and spiky, matching stilettos.

"All Harrows are guilty of something. And it's finally coming out. Cheers." Luna raised her glass in the air and took a swig, only to find it empty. The drunk chef pouted and wandered off.

"If I were a betting cat, I'd lay odds she tops the next body list." Theo, the cat, with a bedazzled track-suit-wearing Horatio the imp on his back, strolled up to Xandie.

"Weren't you boycotting the cocktail party because of my stupid plan to trap a liar and a killer?"

"I was boycotting because it was Lila and Elspeth's plan, and no one made any cat treats." Theo hissed as Horatio yanked on the reins attached to his cat collar. The imp chittered in Theo's ear before taking a kamikaze dive off the cat's back into a still soppy puddle of champagne. Horatio rolled over onto his back, making champagne angels with his arms.

"This offends me on so many levels. Drunk imps are prohibited in my house." Xandie crouched down and fished out Horatio. "I guess my mopping skills are as bad as my sleuthing ones."

"I wouldn't say that, doll-face. This plan of yours is working great." Colin bounced his way over to Xandie's side and lifted his snout in Elspeth's direction.

Xandie followed the tiny dog's nose until she spotted her grandmother, linking her arm around Shan and performing a sneaky swap of champagne glasses.

"She's out of this world sneaky. That Harrow has it going on." Colin approved with a doggy grin.

"The evil witch genius is strong in that one." Xandie rolled her eyes. In an eccentric family, Elspeth stood out as the head wacko, and Xandie shared their gene pool.

"Did she switch them? Did he drink it yet?" Winifred slunk in next to Colin and Xandie, peering around the room.

"The old girl has it in hand." Colin frowned and spun around on the spot, his little nose wrinkling. "Do I smell tuna? Cat food?"

"Put a sock in it, crotch sniffer. You're up at the big house now, not the dog park. Have some manners," Theo hissed back at the pug.

Colin belched and used a paw to scratch his tummy. "Your little feline insults don't impress me since everyone knows you're a fake, anyway."

"A fake?" Theo squeaked the words out, outrage in every quivering whisker. "I am a fur real feline. You are a doggenstein, pug."

Colin growled and prowled toward the cat. "Delinquent Greek teenager."

Theo reared back. "Don't go there, you obnoxious pug."

"Okay, that's it for you two today." Xandie stepped forward and pushed the warring magical animals apart. "Both of you know better."

"He started it," the animals chorused together.

"*Aiii.*" The little imp, drunk on the champagne spill, had somehow found a stray match, lit it, and was now brandishing the match at the dog like a rampaging villager hunting witches with their flaming torches.

Xandie reached forward to grab the match, but it slipped through her fingers and fell smack bang into a puddle of magical over-proofed champagne. Which ignited with a sizzle of blue flame.

Winifred squealed and scrambled for water.

Xandie shoved Theo and Horatio back from the alcoholic blaze.

"See. Delinquent." Colin backed away, shaking his head in disgust.

"It was the imp, not me," Theo roared back.

Horatio danced around the outside of the tiny fire. He shrugged his jacket off and flung it into the air as he danced.

"Oh, for god's sake. Leave you lot alone for a few minutes and you're trying to burn the library down." Elspeth shook her head in disgust. "Wait until everyone leaves and then firebomb it. No witnesses, ladies. Remember, no witnesses." Elspeth pushed Colin out of the champagne fire's path and whispered a word. The sparkling flames snuffed out like exhausted birthday candles.

It was over so quickly most of the guests barely registered the incident.

Horatio moaned and grabbed his jacket, flouncing off in a huff.

Drunk, pyromaniac imps were not part of her get-Shan-to-incriminate-himself plan.

"Any minute now." Elspeth nudged Xandie with a shoulder. "I added a little extra oomph to make sure we'd get him alone."

Knowing her grandmother, the oomph was a laxative. "Tell me you haven't made him sick? I'm not interrogating a man in the bathroom."

"That's amateur work. I'm frying his throat a

little. He'll go searching for water, and then you can nab him." Elspeth pointed at a disappearing Shan. "See? What did I say?"

Xandie ignored Elspeth's antics and followed the Kitsune. Sometimes it was better to ignore her grandmother than get sucked into the chaos and mayhem of the Harrow world of despotic witches.

Slipping inside the kitchen, Xandie caught the door before it slammed shut. Shan hovered by the sink, gulping water straight from the faucet. He spun around to face the door and slurped loose drops of water away from his hand. "Apologies, Ms. Meyers. I think I'm having an allergic reaction to your canapes. My mouth is burning."

Xandie glimpsed his blue tongue as he spoke. Elspeth had assured her the color would wear off in a few minutes. She had to keep asking questions, and while his tongue was blue, he was compelled to answer. Time to test her grandmother's hexing skills. "Sorry to hear that, Mr. Shan. Do you have food allergies?"

"That's an excuse to use when I'm offered substandard food. But this time, I might really be allergic to something."

Shan frowned. He seemed almost taken aback by

his own words. *Elspeth came through.* Xandie prowled toward the kitchen counter. "As long as you're okay. It would be a shame to ruin your trip to Point Muse with an allergy attack. Why did you come here again?"

"I'm a friend..." Shan stuttered to a stop. "Friendly with..." He coughed and then spoke again. "I was asked to meet with Mede Resort."

"Who asked you to come?"

"A secretary working for Hannah Mede, but the meeting was with her husband, Malachi." Shan rubbed his throat, a confused expression on his face.

Xandie cut in with another question before the hex wore off. "Why were you following Hannah around?"

"To make sure she goes ahead with the sale. Malachi said she'd had second thoughts after her office contacted me for a meeting. Point Muse Springs Resort has great potential. Shan Properties Group wants a sale to go through, and Hannah Mede is desperate." Shan sagged against the sink, exhausted.

"Have you spoken to Hannah?"

"Mrs. Mede doesn't want to deal with us directly. We get sent reports."

"Why are they so desperate?"

"Hannah needs to sell. The resort was hers, and she has financial issues. Malachi was a go-between. She's too embarrassed to meet with me and admit she's in debt."

"Hannah's forcing the sale, not her husband?"

"I'm trying to ensure she doesn't change your mind." Shan drank from the faucet again and gurgled before spitting into the sink.

"Would you kill to make sure she sells?"

Another few minutes and the hex would dissipate. She had to know if he was the killer.

Shan breathed deeply and straightened. He brushed down the front of his jacket and narrowed his gaze on Xandie. "Why, Ms. Meyers, anyone would think you were trying to get a confession."

Drat, the hex wore off. No more truthful blue tongue. "Nope, a casual talk with a man drinking out of a faucet."

"Isn't it strange? My tongue started burning, and I felt compelled to answer your every question. How bizarre." He strolled past Xandie and paused in the doorway. "Despite your obvious prodding, I'm happy to talk about the sale of the resort. Anything goes in high-stakes real estate... Anything." He bared his teeth and disappeared into the crowd.

"Well? Did he tell you anything juicy? Did you get a confession?" Elspeth tapped her foot on the tiled floor outside the kitchen.

"The hex wore off just as I asked about the murders. But he was happy enough to offer that anything goes in cutthroat real estate." Xandie clicked her fingers. "Oh, and Hannah's in debt, and she's the one selling with the husband as the go-between."

Lila wandered up as Xandie finished talking, and she shook her head. "It still doesn't sound like her. Plus, she's already told you she isn't a gambler."

"People change. I like her, but we all know people's secrets run deep, especially if they're ashamed."

"Nope. Maybe Elspeth made a mistake on the hex."

"Great. Ask for an old woman's help and then kick her to the cabbages." Elspeth poked her tongue out at her granddaughters. "Faithless child. I feel a sudden need to glue something of yours shut." Elspeth glared at Lila for a moment before offering a wide tooth-filled smile and heading back into the crowd.

Xandie shuddered. "It's the smile. It's worse than a glare."

"You stay away from my good underwear drawer. You hear me, Elspeth Harrow?" Lila ordered her grandmother.

"Do I want to know?"

Lila shuddered. "Last time I questioned my nefarious grandmother's activities, she hexed my underwear drawer shut. Only left me my old laundry day panties. *Never again.*"

Xandie bit back a snicker. All the Harrows had a little drama queen in them, and Lila was worse than Holly for over-the-top dramatics. She almost rivaled their grandmother in the acting stakes.

A long, drawn-out wail sounded from upstairs. Xandie and Lila exchanged a look and then bolted toward the noise.

Hannah Mede crouched on the stairs, shaking a finger pointed upward. "Did you see it? It was her. Oh my God."

Xandie reached down and with Lila's help pulled the trembling woman upright. "Saw who, Hannah?"

"Lulu. Lulu Moon. She was as clear as day, standing at the top of the stairs. I tripped when I saw her." Hannah closed her eyes and hugged her arms tight around her waist.

"Hannah, Lulu's dead. It can't have been her."

Lila rubbed Hannah's back and looked worriedly at Xandie.

Had the stress of everything finally gotten to her, or was Hannah trying to distract them away from death? "Maybe it was the light on the stairs, or you need to eat something," Xandie offered.

Hannah shook off their hands. "I am not blind, hungry, or an idiot. I saw Lulu's ghost. She was pointing a finger at me like she was accusing me of something. Why would Lulu's ghost do that?"

Maybe because Hannah was involved somehow.

"See, you think it's my fault too," Hannah wailed and shoved past the girls into Malachi Mede's waiting arms.

"There, there. I told you last night to get off those shopping sites on the Witchweb. You're probably tired." Malachi steered Hannah toward the front door.

"What? Malachi?" Hannah's confused protest tapered off as the door slammed shut behind them.

Xandie stood next to her cousin. This was Point Muse, weird central. Could it have been a ghost? Was Lulu haunting Hannah?

"Hannah's got a problem." Lila turned a worried face to Xandie.

"That's an understatement." Either Hannah was

a devious killer or a very sick woman. The only other option was Lulu Moon's ghost had unfinished business.

And Hannah is that business...

SIXTEEN

"I told you. Hannah's sleeping before the final pose stage. You can't disturb her." Malachi Mede slapped a hand on his desk and glared at Xandie.

"She was upset last night, and we're concerned about her." Xandie gestured to Elspeth. "This is Elspeth Harrow. She's an expert on hexes and curses, and she can make sure that Hannah's okay."

Malachi Mede roared, "She's already fine. Hannah needs to catch up on sleep. She's addicted to the Witchweb and online shopping and that's all." The fight drained out of the man, and he dropped into his chair behind the desk.

Elspeth harrumphed and jammed her hands on her hips, her purple wig askew. "Suck it up, Mede.

Your wife needs my help. If you love her like you say, let me look at her."

"Fine." Defeated, Malachi pressed the buzzer and spoke into an intercom. His office door opened onto two hulking wolf shifters. "Please get the old witch up to Mrs. Mede. When she's finished, show both these women out. Got me?"

Both shifters nodded and cautiously followed behind Elspeth as she stomped past.

Malachi leaned back in his chair and cleared his throat before glaring at Xandie. "I suppose you have questions for me. I heard from Shan you're a bit of a *Nancy Drew* type."

"Bodies like to turn up in my vicinity. Investigating's my coping skill." Xandie dropped into a chair opposite Mede's heavy wooden desk.

"You need another hobby. One that isn't life-threatening." Malachi glowered at Xandie.

"Is that a threat, Mr. Mede?"

Malachi sighed and ran a hand through his blond curls. "No. It's... I mean..." He leaned back in the chair and stared at the ceiling, words deserting him.

"You're broke. You've got no money, and you need to sell the resort, and Shan is your last chance," Xandie supplied, finishing his sentence for him.

He nodded. "We were good before the resort,

but it was expensive to build on ley lines, and Hannah spent money like wildfire, shopping, gambling. You name it, I've paid for it. Selling the resort is the only option we have to remain afloat. Hannah didn't want anyone in Point Muse to know. I'm the go-between."

He paused and then continued in a lower voice, "She's been a little delicate since it started. The guilt and stress have eaten away at her. She's been having little turns like seeing that ghost last night and even missing periods of time. She keeps blacking out." Malachi banged a fist on the arm of the chair. "The place will sell as soon as the pet show fanatics leave. There's nothing wrong with her that some plain old sleep and no stress won't cure."

"Correct, Mede. There's nothing wrong with Hannah but nerves and tiredness." Elspeth swept back into the room with a shifter on each arm.

"Are you sure?" Xandie frowned at her flirty grandmother, fondling shifter biceps.

"Don't question your elders. You'll live longer." Elspeth patted Xandie on the cheek. "But yes. I'm sure she'll be fine. Besides, we have to go. My source has a name for me. But he won't give it until I trade him my get-up-and-go-go juice recipe."

Xandie rolled her eyes. "Let me guess. The potion is illegal?"

"Well, it ain't sunshine and roses, sweet pea." Elspeth dragged her shifter security guards out the door with her as she left.

"Ms. Harrow saw Hannah, and she's okay. Now leave us alone. That's all we need." He stood and stomped to the door, holding it open for Xandie.

She nodded to Malachi and slid through the door only a few moments before it slammed behind her.

"Awfully fast to get me out of the room," Xandie wondered aloud.

"Are you surprised? You set Elspeth on him. I'd want to get you out of the room too. Or leave screaming myself." Police chief Zach Braun leaned against the wall, opposite Mede's office.

This day was heading nowhere good. "What do you want? You've already arrested my aunt."

"I had no choice, Xandie. With the evidence against Amelia, we had to take her in. You know that."

"She didn't hurt anyone," Xandie replied, cutting off Braun's next words.

"Find some evidence or another suspect and we'll let her go."

"What about that bookie? Or the oh-so-slick Naruto Shan?"

"That bookie Albert Swan? We arrested him last night, on an unconnected matter. Shan's record is spotless, and what kind of motive would he have to kill off the pet show competitors? Find me something or your aunt stays at the precinct." Braun scowled and stomped a few steps away before turning back to Xandie. "And try not to find any more dead bodies." He strode around the corner, out of sight.

That man was a burr on her barnacles. But she kind of agreed with him. More dead bodies weren't on her agenda for the day either. Surviving Colin's last obligatory pose in front of the judges was the only event she had planned.

Xandie winced as Winifred smeared glittery goop over Colin's coat. One dog couldn't support that much chemical enhancement before keeling over, surely. Winifred had been primping him for the last few hours. The posing scheduled over an hour ago had been delayed. A technical hitch. Now the judges planned a late posing and would announce the winner at the party tonight.

"I'm so fine, doll-face." Colin trilled the words to Winifred. "It's my moment to shine like the star I am." He shook off Winifred's sticky hands and pranced around backstage.

"Geez, dog. If your ego gets any bigger, you won't fit up on that stage."

"Xandie, girl, the stage was made for these paws." Colin twitched his bottom at Xandie and let rip with radioactive wind.

Xandie covered her face and moved to the side, letting the green cloud of Colin stink sweep past her.

"Now, now. We can't peak too early. You must present a picture of humility, athleticism, and charisma to the judges." Winifred clapped her hands.

Kill me now. Between Winifred fawning over Colin, the pug's antics, and his radioactive wind, a migraine was clamping Xandie's forehead.

Davros poked his head out from behind the stage curtains. "All ready, Colin?"

"Yes, sir. I'm ready for my spotlight." Colin pranced toward the producer and cocked a leg.

He cleared his throat and sidestepped the pug. "It's a formality. You're the only competitor left standing...alive and kicking, anyway."

"A spotlight is a spotlight, baby. Let me at my fans." Colin panted and stared at the pet show host.

Nodding, Davros disappeared. Xandie heard his muffled tones as the producer cued the host to introduce the last pose and Colin the pug.

"Ciao, bella. It's time to shine." Colin strutted past the curtains and onto the makeshift stage.

Winifred clapped her hands again in support and whispered to Xandie, "I have a lovely meat-flavored surprise for Colin for after it's over. I left it near Lulu Moon's grooming station. She was the only one who had a fridge. Could you please get it for me?"

The last time she had to go fetch for Winifred, she'd found a body. "Does he need any more meat products? That fart earlier was enough to blind me."

"He is an artiste. We need to pamper him."

"Fine." At least it would give her breathing space away from Colin's antics and obnoxious smells. As long as there were no dead bodies to find, she'd be happy.

Xandie backed away from the stage and headed to the grooming tent... *again*. She stepped inside the darkened interior. With all the other competitors dropping out, the quietness screamed at her. She located the fridge, kneeled next to it, and grabbed

Winifred's rabbit flavored treat. She had slammed the door shut and made to stand when a thump of something falling behind the fridge stopped her.

She peered down the back of the fridge and then reached a hand tentatively behind it. Her fingers grasped something hard and square, and Xandie pulled a small glittering pink notebook out. A violent neon heading labeled it *Lorelei LaRue's property*.

"Lorelei's blackmail diary." Xandie pushed her simmering excitement down and flicked through it. There were sporadic posts dotted through the diary. Who wore what, how much better she looked, and what racing corn she'd bet on. Love hearts decorated the entries where she'd backed a winner.

But interspersed with the mundane posts were cryptic comments. "M backed a loser down by eight." Or "P slipped a chem to twitchy." Xandie flipped the page over and sucked in a breath as she read the passage. "Mede desperate. Blondie failed at corns, resort floundering. Ka-ching." Hannah Mede had long flowing gold locks. Could her husband have been right? Had Hannah bankrupted the Mede family with gambling? Could she have killed for this diary?

"Always skulking."

Xandie squealed and flung herself up, diary and

hands pressed against her racing heart. "Seriously, Theo? Is this your plan to send me to an early grave?"

"It's your nosy detective work that will do that." Theo jumped onto a grooming table and twitched an ear at her. "What incriminating evidence has you so engrossed?"

Xandie waved the small diary at the cat and then tucked the little book away in the small of her back underneath the waistband of her pants. "LaRue's diary pictures one of the Medes as desperate. I don't know which one."

"Well, you have other issues to deal with." Theo licked his paw, then groomed his tail, his pet imp, Horatio, absent.

She sagged a little and then took a deep breath. "Fine, what did Elspeth do this time?"

"The police have been chasing a juvenile basilisk around Point Muse. Seems to have slipped its control collar."

"Great." Xandie waved her arms in the air and paced around in a circle. "That's all we need. A rampaging basilisk."

Theo arched his back. "Let's hope it's not teething. Those animals will gnaw anything when a tooth is coming in." He shivered. "I had a run-in with a toddler basilisk once. It chewed on everything it turned to stone. I distracted it with a small animal and ran off."

Xandie rolled her eyes. Theo, her furry coward. *What a surprise.* "How do I deal with it if I come across one?"

"Run away?" Theo hiccupped a furball. "Don't look at it. If you have to, treat it like a Medusa. Look at them through a mirror. Or throw a weasel at it. They can't stand the animals, scare them witless. But that's not the only issue."

"What is?"

"Your grandmother busted your aunt out of jail."

Some days, I can't get a break...

SEVENTEEN

She needed a rest. Five minutes of peace with no rabid killers, devious grandmothers, or prison escapee aunts.

"*Psst*. Xandie. Over here." Hannah Mede, in a hot pink cocktail dress, hid behind a white column, waving her over.

Xandie squinted. She'd looked all afternoon for her escapee family members and found nada. Nothing. Zilch. Then Winifred forced her to dress up and attend Colin's cocktail party crowning. Now she had a murder suspect in a hot pink dress wanting a secret meeting. Her cup runneth over. Xandie slipped in next to Hannah. "You *psst* at me?"

"I found Elspeth and Amelia." Hannah pointed

to the wooded area at the back of the resort. "I went for a walk and found Elspeth and your aunt collecting poisonous mushrooms."

"Why am I not surprised? Did my grandmother say anything?"

"Only '*down with the fuzz.*'" Hannah snickered and then sobered up. "I can show you where they are."

In a dark wood, with a potential killer. Maybe?

Xandie considered Hannah, with her curly blonde locks flowing free and her playful hot pink dress and made a quick decision. No matter the evidence, she was positive Hannah wasn't the killer. "Lead on, Mede, we got jailbait to find."

Xandie and Hannah turned to leave the cocktail party.

"Hey, doll-face, where ya going? Tell me you ain't gonna miss my triumphant win." Colin stood in Xandie's path, gnawing on Winifred's meat present.

"Hannah found Amelia. I'm going after her."

"Miss my win? My crowning?" Colin gasped and shook his rolls in horror.

"First, this isn't a beauty contest. Second, this is family. And that trumps the pet show."

Colin spat out his meat treat and used a claw to

pry food product out of a fang. "Even the glorious Elspeth has deserted me."

Devious, yes. But glorious wasn't a word Xandie would use to describe her grandmother. "Elspeth's with Amelia. We will make sure they're okay."

Lila rushed up. "I've lost contact with Mom and Elspeth. Elspeth scried me, and we were in the middle of yelling, and there was a screech and some kind of flash, and the line went dead."

"Trouble? My Elspeth is in trouble? What are we waiting for?" Colin pawed the ground like an enraged bull. *A pint-sized one.*

"Now you want to leave your own crowning?"

"If my creator's in trouble, that's where I'll be. Besides, Winifred can claim my crown for me." Colin trotted around in a circle, sniffing for a moment, and then called out, "Winifred. Winnie? Here, baby."

Xandie and Lila both gagged at their aunt's new nickname.

"Yes, sweetie? What can I get you?" Winifred appeared out of nowhere and smothered Colin in kisses.

"I'm heading out to rescue Elspeth. Take one for the family and get my award." Colin swiped his tongue over Winifred's cheek. "Let's get this rescue on the road."

A grating, smoke-loving voice suddenly drew Xandie away from the rescue party. "Off on another suspect hunt, Meyers?"

Rogue ASP agent and her mother's chief hound dog stood next to the exit, a cigarette hanging between the fingers of one hand, the other placed conspicuously in a coat pocket.

"I wouldn't be drawing your gun in here, Agent Painful. There are plenty of supernaturals around who would love to deal face to face with an ASP agent. You've probably disappeared some of their family members."

"It's Agent Smith. Remember the name. Because you'll be seeing me again, real soon."

"And you'll be seeing the Harrow family, including my grandmother, Elspeth. She'd love to spend some alone time with you. Now I have something to do that's more important than dealing with pointless innuendo and wannabe bad guy strutting." *Take that, no neck buffoon.*

"Pride, that's what all you Harrows have in common. I'm going to love taking you women down a peg or two. Have fun." He drew his hand out of his coat pocket and pretended to fire an imaginary pistol at Xandie before slinking back into the crowd.

Smith turning up wasn't a good sign. This rescue party would end in disaster. She could feel the ache in her Meyer-Harrow bones.

"I swear they were around here. This is where Amelia told me to come." Hannah squinted into the dark, trying to spy the Harrow runaways.

Lila shook a green crystal until it glowed, illuminating the area. The woods had given way to upward sloping, rocky outcrops, shadowed openings and cliffs.

"Where are we?" Xandie stood with Colin as he nosed around.

"On the border of resort land and the national park. Lots of hikes and caving around here," Hannah offered in the voice of a tour guide.

"And this is where you saw them?" Lila bit her lip.

"Elspeth swore she'd wait here. She told me to hurry and get her ungrateful granddaughters before she hexed my hair dye." Hannah smiled weakly and then trembled. "Sorry. This place creeps me out."

"Don't worry, toots. I've got your back." Colin weaved around Hannah's bare legs.

Xandie grabbed the pug. "Like I didn't see you looking up her skirt then. Give it a rest, dog."

"Quiet, you lot." Lila cocked her head. "Did you hear that?"

The group fell silent. The night carried every noise, including muffled yelling.

"See?" Lila pointed toward some shadowed rocky caves. "Some kind of noise coming from those caves."

"How do you know they're caves?" Xandie peered into the dark, but ominous shadows blanketed their surrounds.

"Bunch of us used to come up here to drink. There are caves right over there." Lila waved a hand.

"It's dark, I can't see anything. Maybe my elderly babe will be fine until morning?"

"Shut up, Colin," the women chorused together.

"Look, I know this place, and I have an extra crystal of Elspeth's." Lila threw her light crystal at Hannah and activated a second one.

"We split up?" This reminded Xandie of the classic stupid high schooler about to die in a cheap horror movie.

"No choice. Use the light and scout around. I'll

let you know if I find anything." Lila blew Xandie a kiss and disappeared into the dark.

Hannah rubbed her arms. "I should've grabbed Malachi before bringing you up here. He'd know what to do."

Xandie picked Colin up, clutched him to her chest. She peered around, trying to spot any sign of her grandmother or aunt passing this way. "No offence, but I think the police chief might've been more use to us."

"You'd be surprised. Malachi's a Medusa descendent. He can't turn anyone to stone but can cast amazing illusions. And he's very knowledgeable on dangerous magical creatures. People sometimes consult him." Hannah gave a proud nod.

"Oh, babe, I wish you hadn't said that." Malachi Mede stepped into the light, carrying a groggy Amelia over his shoulder. He dropped her to the ground and she uttered a low moan.

"Malachi. I'm glad you found us." Hannah rushed forward, a relieved expression on her face, only stopping at Xandie's outstretched hand.

Xandie drew her back, one arm around her and the other holding onto Colin. "I think he's the reason we're out here."

Hannah frowned, confused. "I don't understand."

"Mede's good at illusions. Remember Lulu Moon's ghost on the stairs?" Xandie gripped Colin tight. Elspeth would never forgive her if something happened to her prized pug.

"You had to build a resort here. Wanted to show Point Muse residents how well off you are now." Malachi tugged at a handful of blonde curls. "The ley lines bankrupted us. You insisted we had to come here, and now look at us."

Hannah shook off Xandie's hand. "Why didn't you tell me? I would never have built here if I'd known."

"Why don't you tell her the truth, Malachi?" Xandie dropped Colin, crept over to Amelia, and kneeled next to her aunt. She was alive. Groggy, but still alive. At least Lila had escaped. Hopefully, her impetuous cousin would stay out of trouble and go for help...or at least find their slightly evil grandmother. Xandie straightened and glared at Mede. "You lost on the racing corns big time, didn't you?"

"That damn LaRue found out. We used the same bookie. She wanted money and pretty things to keep her mouth shut. My only option was to sell to

Shan. That would float us until I picked another winner."

"Baby? You lost our money through gambling? Why didn't you tell me?" Tears filled Hannah's eyes as she confronted her husband.

"Because you want a rich husband. You'd have left me if you'd found out." He started pacing as he babbled. "I needed a stake. I know I can pick a winner. The woman was bleeding me, had to shut her up." Malachi flung a shaking hand out, an amulet clenched tightly in the palm of his hand.

Something rustled behind them in the dark. Xandie put two and two together and came up with murder. "You used a basilisk to kill Lorelei."

"She had to go. Someone offered me a basilisk a while ago. They knew

I was an expert in dangerous creatures. It was perfect. All I needed was a control collar."

"And that's why you got rid of me from your office that day. Elspeth was about to find out you were her anonymous buyer."

"I had to get that old bat out of the way before she ruined everything," Mede shouted at Xandie, his face red with fury. "I followed Hannah and overheard your aunt tell her their hiding spot. I had to get here first and deal with them."

What had he done to Elspeth? "Where's my grandmother?"

Malachi smirked at Xandie. "I hit her over the head and left her trussed up in my basilisk's nest. He can deal with her. Silly old bat tried to hex me, but that bleeding heart there on the ground was bleating about saving the basilisk and spoiled the old crow's aim."

Elspeth was devious and had a nasty streak that ran deep. Surely, she could handle an animal whose gaze was certain death?

"Did you kill Lulu and Velma too?" Hannah stood shaking, arms wrapped around her middle.

Malachi put out a hand and ambled toward her, pausing within striking range. "Lulu thought she could pick up where LaRue left off and that fake sidekick, Velma Mystic, had the book. She was ready to announce I was the killer. I didn't have a choice. They both had to go." He grabbed Hannah's hand and drew her toward him. "I know you love this place, but I had to convince you to sell."

Hannah frowned. "All the accidents, that horrible vomiting in the food tent, all the issues with the show. That was you?"

"There's a cancellation clause with the pet people. I tried to get them to cancel, but they were stubborn. Then I thought I could convince you to sell to Shan."

"All this over money? I don't care about cash," Hannah yelled at her dimwit husband. "I loved you, and you caused all those accidents. I could've been hurt." She shook off his hand and shoved him back. "All you had to do was ask. I have money."

Malachi snorted. "Pin money won't help me."

"I invented an alchemy potion for hair loss. I had an offer a few weeks ago. The deal is worth millions. All you had to do was talk to me." Hannah slapped Malachi's chest. "How could you kill people for money? To gamble all our money away? That's disgusting. And you're disgusting."

Malachi roared at Hannah, "Everything I've done was for you." He reached for his wife, but she shoved him away, whacking him with her purse.

"Get away from me."

Xandie tried to step between them, but Malachi grabbed her and shoved her down onto the ground.

"You okay, doll?" Colin snuck over and licked Xandie's face. "Don't get between a married couple when they fight. It's never pretty. Nothing's fair in love, war, and divorce."

"You're a magical dog, Colin. I don't think you qualify as a marriage expert." Xandie rolled over and felt around in the waistband of her smart pantsuit. Thank God she'd ignored Theo's suggestion of a slinky black dress. This way, she could carry Lorelei's little pink diary of incriminating evidence with her. *Maybe a bargaining chip?*

"You're a killer and a gambler. I can't enable you. You need to turn yourself in." Hannah stood with her hands on her hips, scowling at her husband.

Malachi started, and then his eyes narrowed. A gloating smile bloomed across his face. "I can make money. I'll sell this place to Shan, and with your hair potion money, I can have all my debts paid off and start again."

"Hell, no. You do not get my money."

"I do if you have a tragic accident, along with Miss Nosy and her family of meddling hags." Malachi shook his head. "I told you not to go out walking with that dangerous basilisk on the prowl."

Hannah gasped. "You wouldn't dare."

"I'm in with multiple bodies, what's a few more?"

Xandie pushed herself up. "I object to being a future body."

"How are you going to stop me?" Malachi smirked.

"I have Lorelei's diary, detailing all her dealings with you and others. It's pretty incriminating."

Malachi's face contorted with rage. "Give it to me now."

"Release Hannah and my Aunt Amelia first."

He raised the amulet that had lain dormant in his fist and concentrated for a moment before staring back at her. "I could take the book from your stony bones instead."

Hannah screeched as the rustling behind Xandie grew louder and her husband's smile grew bigger…

Until Elspeth and Lila emerged into the light, matching amber Harrow eyes glinting with malice.

Elspeth posed at the edge of the light from her glow stone. "Wow, look at what I've found. A nasty murderer and my beautiful prizewinning pug."

"You have nine lives, old woman. But I'm happy to end them all." Malachi raised his amulet at Elspeth.

"No more killing." Hannah raised her purse and threw it at her husband's head.

He howled and stumbled back.

Clapping her hands at her aim, Hannah crowed, "Never leave home without a heavy science text or two. Great for hitting some sense into your murderous husband's thick skull."

Elspeth raised a hand and threw a handful of glittering dust into the air, causing tiny fireworks to explode over Malachi's head.

Not wanting to miss out on the action, Xandie grabbed Lorelei's pink book and waved it in the air as bait. She noticed an ominous shadow move behind Malachi, out of range of the light.

Malachi stopped wailing as his gaze narrowed on the book in Xandie's hand.

Xandie threw the book over his head, and it landed next to the suspiciously moving shadow.

Malachi spun about, intent on reaching the diary...until he stumbled over a belching Colin.

He flew backward, his arms flailing in the air as he met the ground with a thunk. "I will kill that damn dog for that." He rolled over onto all fours as the shadow ambled into the light.

The size of a large dog, the shadow resolved itself into a juvenile basilisk. A cockerel's feathered head placed atop a stout body and spindly chicken legs, with tattered dragon wings and a serpent's tail completed the image of a deadly killer.

A killer who was staring straight at the murderous Malachi Mede.

Xandie clapped a hand over her mouth as a rotting, putrid stench rolled over the women.

Mede shuddered, his back elongated and his fingers clawed the ground until they slowed and finally stopped. Malachi Mede, frozen in stone, toppled onto his side.

Hannah screamed and closed her eyes, trying to block the basilisk stare as it shuffled forward and started nibbling on Mede's ear.

"Well, karma sure does love a practical joke." Elspeth cackled and picked up the control amulet. She whistled at the basilisk and snapped on the collar as it brushed against her legs. Colin belched and trotted over to Elspeth, who picked him up and cooed, "Who's my big boy? You are. Yes, you are." Elspeth nuzzled the pug before shoving him at Xandie and wandering over to a still bound and gagged daughter.

Amelia thumped her feet on the ground and glared at her mother over her gag.

"Have to remember Mede's technique. This is the quietest you've been since you were born." Elspeth guffawed but pointed an accusing finger at her daughter. "And if you ever spoil my hex aim again, I'll make sure you taste salt for the rest of your life." Sniffing, Elspeth turned, collected Hannah, and strutted down toward the resort, the basilisk following along behind.

Xandie sighed as she dropped Colin next to Lila and untied her aunt.

Amelia glared down the hill at her mother's disappearing back. "That woman is a menace, and it galls me she had to waddle to the rescue."

Xandie commiserated. Her grandmother was an amazing woman but with an ego as big as her reputation. Combine that with her unhealthy fascination with hexes, and she wasn't a person you wanted to cross. "At least you aren't a basilisk chew toy." Both women spared a glance for a now earless Malachi Mede statue.

"True, but we still won't hear the end of it." Amelia massaged her freed wrists. "All those poor people and animals killed for money." Amelia shook her head. "That's why I stay away from the pet circuit. Greed and shallow people don't mix."

A Harrow never spoke truer words. The murderer was dead, victims avenged, and her aunt's name cleared... And still her grandmother laughed as she marched back to the resort.

Lila held up her spelled phone. "I got through to Aggie. She's sending the chief up to collect Mede and the basilisk."

Police Chief Braun. Always late to the party when the Harrow witches were involved. At least this time she wouldn't have to put up with his lecture on staying out of a crime scene. He'd wanted her to produce a suspect other than her aunt, and she'd served him up a stone cold one.

Another day in body central, Point Muse, done and dusted.

EIGHTEEN

Xandie gagged and blocked her nose as Colin cleared the morning's breakfast of bacon, beans, and eggs out of his system.

"Better out than in, baby girl. Besides, I have a delicate system." Colin rubbed his belly and rolled on the ground at the base of Harrow House's front stairs.

"I swear Elspeth gets more hag-like the older she gets." Lila sprawled over the top step, wrinkling her nose at Colin's antics.

"Colin's the last in a lengthy list of misdemeanors. I'm surprised no one's put a hit out on her yet."

Hannah giggled at Xandie and swung her feet up underneath her as she settled into the porch swing.

Xandie smiled as she watched Hannah relax. The last few days had taken a toll on the former Point Muse resident. Finding out your husband was a killer and planned to take you out too had to damage her psyche. But somehow Hannah had stepped out of the mental shadows and emerged a happier person. The police had closed the case of the pet show murders and shipped the basilisk to a magical zoo. Hannah had sold her resort to the Point Muse Council for a knockdown price and pulled out of her hair tonic deal. She'd partnered with Amity Puffin to mass-produce it themselves for the supernatural world. Odds were, they'd make a killing. *Pun intended.*

The only loose tie was ASP and their chief idiot, Agent Smith. After delivering his message, the government agents and their stereotypical black SUV were noticeably absent from Point Muse. Elspeth had told her when she moved to Point Muse to keep her enemies close enough that she could dose them with a nasty itching hex if need be. Disappearing ASP agents made her teeth hurt. As for her mom, Herman, her troll private investigator, had been silent on the subject of Miranda Harrow, nary an invoice sent for work rendered. She was secretly relieved. Her emotions were mixed when she thought of her long absent mother.

"Please, I'm at the top of everyone's hit list." Elspeth snorted as she sailed onto the porch with a lime green concoction in hand that had smoke curling around the straw. "I'm that good." She cackled, and a bolt of thunder boomed in the distance.

Lila rolled her eyes. "She times it that way, makes her look more wicked witch."

Xandie snickered from her perch next to the stairs, her angst forgotten. The Harrows were chaotic and argumentative and breathed mayhem, but they weren't boring.

The screeching sound of an abused pink moped tearing down the street outside of Harrow House had their squabbling grinding to a halt.

Amelia and Winifred stepped out of the house, both frowning, as Holly skidded to a stop in front of the stairs.

Xandie straightened, it was never a good sign when her banshee cousin came running. "What's wrong, Holly?" Part banshee and part witch, her cousin's powers always frizzed in and out. *At least until recently.*

Holly raised her head, and her eyes glowed ruby

red with silver rings. She took a trembling step forward, her head dropped back, and an undulating wail rose from her.

That is new. Her cousin's eyes normally bled silver, and she'd never wailed before. Xandie winced as the noise scraped at her nerves. She glanced around, hoping for answers, but her family looked as confused as she was. Holly's cry snapped off, and she lowered her chin. Her gaze snagged Elspeth, and Holly's finger, now tipped with a silver claw, pointed straight at her grandmother's heart.

Everyone looked between Holly and Elspeth, locked in a banshee versus witch stare-down. The flapping of wings and the caw of crows overhead broke the deadly staring contest.

Holly blinked furiously and lowered her fingers as Elspeth started down the stairs toward her.

Something brushed past Xandie's head, and she ducked. The crow cawed again as it fluttered into the air in front of them before stiffening and dropping like a stone at her grandmother's feet.

Elspeth wore a mask of pain. She threw her cocktail, glass and all, into the shrubs at the side of the house and squatted beside the crow. She placed her hand on its chest, trying to feel for a heartbeat. After a moment, Elspeth moved her hands away and stood. Like a bone-weary old woman, she wobbled up the stairs and slammed the front door behind her.

Her daughters, Amelia and Winifred, shared a worried glance and followed her into the house.

Hannah stopped the swing with a toe and shifted her gaze between the front door and Xandie and her cousins.

Lila arrowed a worried gaze at Xandie before rubbing Holly's back.

"I couldn't stop it. Couldn't stop the scream." Holly's face crumpled as she delivered the ominous words. "It's Elspeth. Death is coming for her *and soon.*"

Xandie joined her cousins and gave them a quick group hug. "Elspeth eats death for breakfast."

"*Not this time.*" Holly shut the conversation down.

She'd found her Harrow grandmother and as quirky and as devious as Elspeth was, there was no way Xandie would let her go now. She was the *librarian* and, according to Elspeth, a catalyst. Bodies were her business, and now it was personal.

The only problem? Living up to the Harrow blood line might be the death of her...

The End...

Book Four, The Cursed Crow and the Deadly Hex
is available on Amazon now!

NEWSLETTER

Want more?

You can sign up for my mailing list. It's for new releases and no spam. Be the first to grab specials, new releases, and freebies.

Sign up now.
https://www.kellyethan.com/newsletter

ABOUT THE AUTHOR

I want to thank everyone who spent the time to read my novel.

My world is small town magic, mystery and mayhem, with plenty of snarky laughs along the way.

With an overactive imagination and a love of all things that go bump in the night, it was natural to write cozy paranormal mysteries, but I also love paranormal romance. No matter the genre, I love sarcastic heroines who like to save the day and solve the puzzle.

With a busy and chaotic household, writing is my outlet for madness. I live in Australia and when not writing, I can be found plotting my next fictional murder or chasing after the family's ferocious hellhound.

Visit me today at my website or say hello on
Facebook or Twitter.

Website:
https://www.kellyethan.com

Banshee, Vikings and Voodoo

#1 Banshee, Death and Disarray

#2 Banshee, Moonshine and Madness

#3 Banshee, Sea Monster and Sabotage

HOLLY HARROW Point Muse Boxed Set: Books 1-3

Non Fiction

Heart and Craft.